The Independent Bookworm

About the Book

Soon after the Chinese declare war, Lydia notices that the American dragons need a royal leader if they're to survive. Now she's facing the choice of saving her dragons and abandoning Colin or vice versa.

Also, she bears the burden of a timid Chinese dragoness with little self-esteem who is obviously falling for the last trained dragon hunter. The problem with that? The dragon hunter has been born female.

And her friend Nicole is no help either since she still can't control her overflowing magic. She's a catastrophe waiting to happen.

What are Lydia and her friends are going to do to stop the war, punish the traitors, and bring peace to all of dragonkind? Will they be able to hold on to their loved ones when the whole world seems to have turned against them?

About the Author

Ever since she was born, Katharina Gerlach had her head in the clouds. She and her three younger brothers grew up in the middle of a forest in the heart of the Luneburgian Heather. After romping through the forest with imagination as her guide, the tomboy learned to read and disappeared into magical adventures, past times or eerie fairytale woods.

She never returned to Earth for long, although she managed to successfully finish training as a landscape gardener, study forestry and gain a PhD. But then, she discovered her vocation: storytelling and realized she'd have to write to make her dream of sharing her stories with others come true.

Katharina loves to write Fantasy, Science Fiction and Historical Novels for all age groups. At present, she is writing at her next project in a small house near Hildesheim, Germany, where she lives with her husband, three children and a dog.

more information: www.KatharinaGerlach.com

Crowned by Fire

Katharina Gerlach
and Leonie Joy

Crowned by Fire
published by the Independent Bookworm, USA und D
This book is also available as eBook. It has been published in English and
in German.

If you find any typos or formatting problems in this eBook, please contact
the publisher (www.IndependentBookworm.de).
printed On-Demand Publishing LLC, 100 Enterprise Way, Suite A200,
Scotts Valley, CA 95066, USA, www.createspace.com

ISBN-13 978-3-95681-134-0

More information can be found on the publisher's website:
http://www.IndependentBookworm.de

For my family. I couldn't have done it without you.

TABLE OF CONTENTS

HIGH SCHOOL DRAGONS 1: KISSED BY FIRE
Fantasy Romance

It's highly recommended to read the trilogy's previous volumes first.

The flames of a car crash have killed Lydia's parents and erased her former life from her mind. To be able to go on, she seals her emotions in a hidden corner of her mind. She no longer cares that she's got to live with a foster mother or that she must to go to school again. The world has lost all color, all scent, and all sense.

But on her first day in Hilldale High School, she meets two young men that break through her barriers. Harm—strong, dark, and strangely old-fashioned—lights up her senses. And then, there's Colin, whose gentle jokes and easy camaraderie soothe her soul and fill her with peace.

When a waste paper basket spontaneously ignites on its own, Lydia begins to dream of dragons. Will she be able to find out who she is and what she wants before her past catches up with her?

available as eBook and in print
ISBN-13 978-3-95681-091-6

HIGH SCHOOL DRAGONS 2: TRIED BY FIRE
Fantasy Romance

To live her life as a normal human, Lydia has to catch up on several years of school. However, the dragon's Council insists she become their queen—without Colin. For the sake of peace, Lydia agrees to a visit of the dragon's realm, to reconnect with their way of life. At the same time she find a tutor because giving up on her dreams is not an option.

Colin worries whether he's ready for the love of a dragoness. Can he, as a human, do justice to a relationship this early in his life? Or is he doomed to hurt Lydia one day?

Although Harm takes care of his biological father, Blackfeather, he avoids talking to him. How is he supposed to handle all the lies Blackfeather had to tell him over the years? And then there's Nicole who slowly but inevitably captures his heart although she still fights the idea that dragons or magic exist.

And Mordekay too hasn't given up on his plans. He simply adjusted them to the new situation. Now humanity's freedom and the survival of a whole species are under threat. Can the friends defeat him permanently without forcing Lydia to accept the crown?

available as eBook and in print
ISBN-13 978-3-95681-110-4

PROLOG

As Sun Min left the village behind, the houses huddled together like chickens surrounded by foxes, she breathed the icy air with delight. It tasted of snow – a lot of it, which was confirmed by the mass of dark clouds hanging over the wide valley that connected two mountains high enough to kiss the sky.

Just like Chen and me, she thought. A tiny smile tugged at the corners of her mouth, mirroring the wind that pulled at her simple woolen coat. She let it drop to the ground and enjoyed the north wind's caress on the pale skin of her naked arms. How she'd missed walking in a light shift on a day like this. Had she really been so besotted with Chen that she'd forgotten her first love? Well, her swollen belly answered that question without a doubt.

Kicking off her shoes, she gasped as the soles of her feet touched the needle-like spikes of last year's grass, frozen by the wind's breath. She started to climb. Like a sleepwalker, she found her way higher up the craggy slopes of the northern mountain. The need to reach the part where life clung to tiny gaps in seas of rock and stone pulled her along.

Her flexible toes dug into the smallest fissures as she climbed the steep slope, keeping her grounded while the wind played with her long, black hair, growing wilder by the minute.

When the clouds split and hurled tiny ice crystals toward the ground, she stopped and put her head back to look up at the whirling, coiling mass. With a happy sigh she stuck out her tongue and tried to catch the star-shaped wonders.

One snowflake settled on the palm of her left hand like an icy kiss while others condensed around her into a gown she hadn't worn for way too long. She hadn't expected a welcome like this. A tear, driven by nostalgia, formed on her cheek, freezing before it could roll over her skin. She wiped it away. It felt good to be home.

Buffeted by winds gusting from every side and surrounded by a cloud of snowflakes, she found the perfect spot. Snow drifted gently over a flat granite depression the size of Chen's bed. It was surrounded by boulders that kept the howling of the winds at bay just enough that a newborn wouldn't be scared by it. Sun Min turned into her dragon form and curled up on the coarse stone. The snow arranged itself around her in soft pillows and blankets.

As the snow reached the village she'd left behind, the humans' fear rode on the winds and filled her with pain that joined the first pangs of labor. The snowstorm filled her and her world – the perfect weather for the birth of her daughter.

FIRST CHAPTER

*C*olin's hand clenched around the makeshift sword. Although the metal was bent and dented after Harm had destroyed the cage they'd been in, it had enough ragged edges and sharp spikes to hurt a dragon. And Colin intended to use it for exactly that purpose.

If they've harmed Lydia, I'll hunt them down until they're dead. His eyes narrowed, and he tapped his foot impatiently, watching White Crow examine the ground thoroughly.

"Mordekay and Telanuel flew. Their tracks end right there." The Native American pointed to the left to a steep, rocky incline where flowering perennials clung desperately to what little soil they found between the stones. "They're most likely in another hideout already. But the little dragon went that way." He pointed along the low rise leading over a rocky plateau. Softly rolling meadows fell away on the right.

"Her scent is quite strong," Herbert confirmed. He had used the excellent nose of his pink dragon body. "She went on foot."

Without hesitation, Colin stormed forward, barely noticing that Luke fell in at his side. For a while, they ran up the gentle

13

slope silently where the grass was just turning from yellow to green. Spring had definitely begun to change this part of the world too. The carpet of colorful blooms was heartwarming, but Colin had no eyes for it. His only thoughts belonged to Lydia in her predicament. *I'll save you,* he promised her in thought. *I might not be as strong as a dragon, but I'll save you.* Huffing, he tried to run even faster.

"It's kinda interesting that Meiming decided not to fly," Luke said.

Colin envied the girl knight her stamina. She wasn't the slightest bit out of breath yet. He kept his answer short to preserve air. "Didn't know she could." After all, the lithe, white Chinese dragon that had kidnapped Lydia had no wings, just a few blueish hairs on her legs and a blue-green horizontal frill on both sides of her spine.

"I wonder if Lydia's unconscious body is too heavy for her." Luke pulled ahead. "She's such a frail creature, always bullied by Mordekay. And Telanuel never stopped him, although he's her legal guardian."

"Don't care." Colin pumped his leg muscles to catch up again. His lungs burned, his stomach clenched at the thought of losing Lydia, and his fingers hurt from clutching the makeshift sword, but his goal was clear. "I'll kill her."

"I can't let you." Just as Luke turned to look at Colin, Herbert's small, pink, rotund dragon body overtook them.

"Boys, you've got to let the others catch up." His voice was surprisingly loud. "Harm's still hurting. They're not as fast as you are."

Colin just snorted—just as much to Herbert's words as to Luke's. He'd catch that Chinese dragon, kill it, and save Lydia.

14

Lowering his head and drawing his temporary weapon closer, he tried to run even faster despite his burning lungs.

"Stop!" Luke's warm arms encircled Colin's legs, and he slammed face first onto the stony ground. Pain shot through his body but to his surprise, he hadn't bitten his tongue or bumped his nose. He looked up to scold Luke. Instead, his jaw dropped.

A body-length in front of him, the world stopped. In his frenzy to save Lydia, he'd nearly overlooked the cliff where the grassy plateau ended. *Noooo.* His mind was awash with horror scenarios. What if the Chinese dragon really couldn't fly? Or if she could, what if Lydia was too heavy? What if Mordekay or Telanuel had been waiting for them? They'd been dead set on murdering Lydia. Colin feared the sight at the bottom of the cliff. What was he to do?

Meiming concentrated as best she could. Flying with the dead weight of the girl in her front limbs was hard enough. The magic she needed to keep in the air had always been slippery, but right now if felt soaked in soap. And her anxiety didn't help either. Where was Telanuel? And who were the golden and white dragons pursuing Mordekay?

Meiming forced more magic into her flying spell to speed up, but the black shape inevitably drew away from her. *Wait for me!* She wanted to scream, but had no air for that. She would be faster if she could set down the girl, but Telanuel would be so disappointed if she didn't bring her, and she didn't want to upset him. Anyway, if she stopped, Mordekay would be completely out of sight.

She clutched the girl closer to her chest and gazed down at the ground speeding past. That always calmed her. The tree-studded landscape looked like the accessories of the toy train her mother had given her on her seventh birthday. *Oh Mom, if only you were still here* … She recalled her wide, white furred face with the two, red mustache-like tendrils on either side of the tooth-studded jaw. How she missed her warm embrace, the caress of her clawed paws, their secret flying sprees at night, when the humans slept and Telanuel was out of town. There was the lump in her throat again.

Meiming swallowed and concentrated on Mordekay again. He was zigzagging to evade his pursuers, which gave Meiming a chance to catch up. Sucking in air to get rid of the lump, she concentrated harder to fly faster. She'd have to do something about the white and gold dragons soon or Telanuel would accuse her again of not liking his friend. Although that was true, Meiming didn't want to disappoint him. If only she could reach the fiends with her Commanding Voice.

Mordekay resembled a black bolt of lightning as he shot from left to right and back. The tang of his panic rode on the wind, worrying Meiming. Did he even know where he was flying? Had Telanuel told him where they would meet?

The white and gold dragons pursuing him flickered, and Meiming hadn't done anything to cause that. What the…? The girl in Meiming's arms moaned, so she clutched her closer to her chest to stop her from slipping. It wouldn't do to let her drop. The two dragons flickered again. There … not there … Meiming blinked. How did they do that?

The girl moaned some more and began to twitch. Drat. A moving human, was so much harder to carry. Meiming looked around for a place where she could set her down; something like a rocky needle where she could leave her until Telanuel came to fetch her, but there was nothing suitable close by.

The two dragons winked out of existence. Meiming's jaw dropped. Suddenly the girl jerked awake and slipped. Meiming tried to pull her closer, but the flailing arms made it hard to hold onto her.

Mordekay seemed to have realized that his pursuers were gone. He sped up and headed straight for the horizon. So he *did* know where Telanuel had gone.

"Wait for me!" Meiming's words were barely more than a whisper. Instinctively she reached for the retreating black dragon with one of her front paws, letting go of the girl. What would she do if she lost him? She didn't have a clue where Telanuel went. She had to get rid of the ballast. Opening her other paw, she dropped the girl, extending a little magic to gently float her down. But the human screamed, grabbed a hind leg, and curled around it. Meiming's concentration broke, and together they toppled toward the ground.

When I woke, two white dragon paws held me as the ground rushed past below me. The Chinese girl … Memories flooded my brain. Mordekay cutting himself … the gigantic jaws with the spiky teeth hanging over Blackfeather's limp body … the iron cage in the cave … my parents' magically resurrected forms hurtling after Mordekay …

One paw let go, and I tried to focus. Would the Chinese dragon be able to carry me with only one paw?

"Careful, hon," Mom's voice rang in my ear, mirroring my worry.

"We love you," Dad said.

I felt them slip back into the realm of Queen's Magic where they belonged, and a part of my heart went with them.

The second paw released me. My scream shrilled through the air and I grabbed instinctively for something to hold onto. My arms closed around a scaly pole with soft hairs that flapped into my face—the Chinese dragon's hind leg—before I realized that I hadn't been in danger. There had been magic around me that would have taken me down to the ground sedately. But it was gone.

Now, we were both hurtling toward the ground. The Chinese dragon's shriek pierced my ears. Wind ripped at my clothes, and the ground rushed toward us. I did the only thing I could think of: I shifted.

My big wings caught the wind, and pain lanced from my shoulders through my body. Ignoring my protesting muscles, I flapped my wings as best I could. We slowed but were still too fast for a soft landing. However, I would not let the other dragon go. She had a lot of questions to answer.

Just before we reached the ground, I curled up around the much smaller white dragon. Our crash shook the only tree in the vicinity and arolla pine cones rained down on us. I gasped for air but still clung to the Chinese dragon.

It didn't move. Was she hurt badly? That couldn't be. I'd cushioned her fall as best I could. When I looked closer, I noticed that she was pressing her eyes shut. A smile tugged at my mouth. It reminded me of some of my childhood friends who used to pretend they were invisible by closing their eyes. Much more gentle than I meant to, I said, "You can stop pretending. I know you're awake."

"Please don't kill me." The Chinese dragon curled up even more.

"I'm not going to kill you." I was appalled. Who had told her I'd kill her? That wasn't my style. I shook my head. I didn't need a style. I wasn't going to be queen anyway. Still, I couldn't simply let her go. "But you do realize that my friends are quite annoyed with you."

"I haven't done anything." The white ball shrank even more if possible, and the voice sounded muffled. "I only helped Pa when he had things to carry."

"Pa?" Surely she wasn't related to Mordekay.

"Well, Telanuel isn't really my father, only my legal guardian." The dragon relaxed a little. "And he'll be here any minute to pick me up."

"I don't think so." Shifting back into human shape, I pointed to the sky where Harm's big form followed by Herbert's much smaller one were heading toward us.

The white, scaly ball began to shiver. I felt a little sorry for her, but maybe the fear she felt now would loosen her tongue when we returned to the castle.

Colin ground his teeth. Even from a distance, the deep, dragon-shaped dent in the earth was impressive. It showed clearly that Lydia was too nice by far. She'd actually tried to save her kidnapper. He shook his head. And what did she get? Pain, most likely. The crash had been loud enough to alert White Crow and Herbert to Lydia's whereabouts. His gaze clung to the small figure that was sitting at the indentation's rim, hugging her knees.

The minute Harm set down on the green-tinged grass beside Lydia, Colin jumped off. He felt Luke's fingers grab for him, but he was too fast to be held back.

Raising his makeshift sword, he rushed toward the Chinese dragon, screaming at the top of his lungs. He wanted her to feel Lydia's pain, very single muscle ache, and his too. Nothing in his life had been as bad as not knowing where his love was.

But before he could shove the tip of his sword into the white ball, Lydia grabbed his arm. "Leave her alone. Please. For me."

He turned with tears in his eyes, dropped the weapon, and slung his arms around her. Sobs racked his body, and he clung to her as if he were drowning. "I'm sorry," he whispered. "I'm so sorry. I'll never let anything happen to you again. Ever!"

"Colin, I love you." Her words soothed his soul, and he finally stopped shivering. "But I'm perfectly capable of defending myself, especially against someone so much smaller than I am. I'm not a princess." She giggled. "Well, I guess, technically I am. Still, I'm not *that* kind of princess."

Still hugging, they sat down and kissed, oblivious to the coldness of the ground. Breathing in her familiar scent of burnt vanilla and with her white-blonde hair tickling his nose, Colin finally calmed down. Her lips on his caused electrical currents to run through his body. How he'd missed that. Already he was dreaming of a wedding ceremony, although his parents would surely insist they wait a couple of years and finish high school first.

"Lydia Concordia Draconia Dragonis!" White Crow's voice sounded stern. "We've certainly got more important things to do than smooching."

Reluctantly, Colin let Lydia go. He marveled at how regal she looked when she turned toward her former mentor. "This was important. Colin needs to be clear-headed, not a shivering mess." Then she smiled. "I'm glad you're here though. And you too, Herbert."

"Any time." The tiny dragon shifted into his old man's body and winked at her before pointing to the Chinese dragon. "What are we going to do with the girl?"

"Her name's Meiming," Luke said, glaring at Herbert.

The old man smiled. "We still need to decide what to do with her. We can't leave her to Mordekay."

"We'll take her along," Lydia hooked her hands over Colin's arm, which sent a pleasurable shiver through his body. "Mordekay and Telanuel are gone for now, but they'll be back, I'm sure. It'd be best to find out where they hide so we can take precautions."

Harm chimed in. "And Nicole and Blackfeather need protection. Angie took them to your parents' house, and Mordekay knows where that is."

An unpleasant thought occurred to Colin, and he said, "Don't forget that spring holidays will be over soon, and we'll be expected back home."

Luke and Harm moaned, but Lydia grinned happily. Did she like school? What an amazing girl … *his* girl!

"Fine," she said. "Harm, you'll protect Nicole and Blackfeather. Take White Crow with you. He's the best help. Colin, Luke and I will take Meiming to the castle." How easily Lydia commanded the others. She was the born Queen. Colin swallowed at what it would mean for him if she really accepted the crown, but pushed the thought aside when Lydia continued to speak. "You should go with them too, Herbert. It's best that Meiming doesn't see another dragon for a while. After all, she can use Queen's Magic, and we need to find the reason for that. If she turns out to be of royal blood, she'll be a valuable asset in the coming war."

"War?" Colin's head snapped up as if someone had slapped him. "What war?"

"The Chinese dragons declared war. I'll explain that later." She shifted into her dragon form. "We'll meet the others at my parents' house as soon as we've made sure neither Mordekay nor Telanuel can steal her from under our noses. Hop on, Colin."

War! Colin climbed onto Lydia's back without seeing anything of his surroundings. War meant death and destruction. It also meant that humans would probably discover that dragons still existed. And then, the hunt would begin. He swallowed, but his throat had gone dry. How long would the Chinese need to get to the American dragons' village in the mountains? Would that be enough time for Luke to teach him how to fight?

Trembling a little, he slipped forward a bit to make room for Luke, who put her arms around him. The hardness of the makeshift sword pressed into his back. Was Luke taking it along? Well, it might be a wise move, considering that Meiming might find the strength to break Lydia's commands.

"Meiming, uncurl!" Lydia's order vibrated in Colin's bones. She must be using strong magic. "Fly with me and do everything I say without comment. Understood?"

"Yes." Meiming's voice was so low, Colin nearly missed her answer, but she uncurled and readied herself for takeoff.

Second Chapter

They reached the dragon castle without incident. The platform in front of the facade that had been cut out of the rock was empty. Where were all the dragons? The corridors inside were empty too. Lydia didn't shift into her human form, which Colin thought a good idea. This way her much bigger body would be a good shield should another dragon show up. But they marched through deserted corridors filled only by a low murmur that rumbled through the tunnels. Had all the dragons gathered somewhere to discuss the coming war? Colin shivered at the thought of dragon fighting dragon. What would happen to the humans in the vicinity? And how would the military react to that? The coming war could well be the end of the dragons.

With the hallways devoid of humans and dragons, they made good progress. Only once did Lydia have to tell a nosy guard to forget them and go someplace else. To Colin's surprise, Lydia took them to the truth chamber. A big boulder had been placed over the entrance, but Lydia rolled it aside without much trouble. Inside, nothing had changed. The pile of gold was still there. How clever of Lydia! Hopefully the magic that forced anyone in the chamber to speak the truth would be strong enough to compel someone who might have royal blood.

"Stay here," Lydia commanded and Meiming rolled up on the pile of gold.

Luke stepped closer and turned to face Lydia. "I'll stay with her. She'll need someone to fetch food or water."

Lydia nodded. "I'll let the other dragons know that you're allowed to come and go as you please." She returned to her human form and walked up to the Chinese dragon's nose. "How come you can use Queen's Magic?"

Meiming frowned, which made the hairs on her head stand up. "I don't know what you're talking about."

That couldn't be the truth. Colin was sure about it. Of course she would know what kind of magic she was using. So the magic of the chamber wasn't strong enough after all.

"Try telling me your name is Karl." Lydia used the Commanding Voice. Obviously she was thinking along the same lines but had figured out a way to test the truth spell's strength. Colin grinned at her ingenuity. If the Chinese dragon managed to speak the lie as instructed, and he was sure she would, they would know for sure that the chamber's spell wasn't strong enough.

To his surprise, Meiming opened and closed her mouth but nothing came out. Her body began to twist and shudder. Caught between two equally strong spells, she wasn't able to obey either.

"Do something!" Luke stared at Lydia with his hands balled to fists. "This'll kill her."

Hurriedly, Lydia said in the Commanding Voice, "Disregard my last order."

Meiming relaxed but she was breathing hard. Luke patted her shoulder, still glaring at Lydia. Colin was dumbstruck. Meiming was really telling the truth? How could she not know what kind of magic she was using?

Lydia looked as shocked as he felt. "You really don't know that you've got magic much stronger than that of an average dragon?"

"Yes, I do. I'm a freak in every regard." Meiming put a paw over her face, probably to hide tears.

"You're not a freak!" Luke blurted out. "You're the most beautiful dragon I ever met."

Lydia grinned. "Oh, the chamber seems to be working on humans too." Well, Colin could have told her that before. Lydia went on. "Luke is right. You're not a freak at all."

"But Mordekay—"

"Regardless what anyone else said," Lydia didn't let her interrupt, "you're a Chinese dragon with all the features the species has, that's why you look so different."

Meiming's eyes widened.

"And for some reason you can use Queen's magic. We'll have to examine that soon, but right now I'm hard pressed for time." Lydia put her hands on her hips. "Your magic's not as strong as mine, but much stronger than that of any other dragon. Therefore I need you to stay here and not talk to anyone but Luke. Will you promise, or do I have to Command you?"

Lydia trusted a kidnapper's word? Colin's hands grew cold. Was that wise?

"I promise by my mother's grave." Meiming bowed her head.

Lydia's eyes widened. "Grave? She wasn't burned? Or did the dragon part come from your father?" Meiming opened her mouth as if to answer, but Lydia waved at her. "No, don't answer that. We'll get to those details when I come back to find out why you can use Queen's Magic."

Meiming's mouth closed with a thud.

Luke turned to Lydia. "I would offer my help for the war against the dragons, but I cannot fight against Meiming's people. It doesn't feel right. And also, I've got to adjust my view of the world. So many of my perceptions have proven wrong and I still haven't had time to think things through properly."

"I'll take Colin to the others and we'll let you know what you can do once we've figured out some plans. Okay?" Lydia smiled and Colin's right hand balled into a fist. How could she gift another person with that? He bit his lip and forced his fingers to open. Lydia could smile at whoever she chose. She was his girlfriend, not a slave, and he wanted her to have friends beside him. And if he took Angie's words seriously, which he did, Lydia would never love anyone but him anyway, so there was no reason at all for jealousy. But it was hard.

The smile Lydia gave him was especially mellow and full of love. "Can we go?"

Luke watched them leave the cave hand in hand. Lydia didn't put the stone that had covered the entrance back into place, and she was grateful for that. She sat down on the ground, which was surprisingly cold. Well, a knight coped with that wordlessly, as her father had told her. She sighed. There were so many things that she hadn't known, things she should have known as a dragon hunter.

"Thank you for staying with me," Meiming said. "I've never been alone for more than an hour in my whole life. It scares me."

"I won't leave you if I don't have to." Luke was surprised at the heat rolling though her body at those words. What would her father think if he knew how protective she felt about a dragon? It didn't matter than she'd admired Meiming from afar for quite a while, she was a *dragon*. A Chinese dragon, but a dragon nonetheless.

A timid smile played around Meiming's mouth. "Still, thank you. I didn't think you'd still be my friend after the way Dad and Mordekay treated you."

"That wasn't your fault." Luke shifted a little. The ground wasn't just cold, it was hard. Sitting hurt after a while.

"I tried to tell them to leave you alone, but they are both trained at ignoring my Commanding Voice." Meiming slid her tail off the pile of gold and fanned out the hair-covered fin at the end. "You seem uncomfortable. Please sit here. I won't feel it."

Drat, Luke thought. *Still the sissy, the girl.* "If only I'd been born a boy." Oh dear, why had she said that?

Meiming lifted an eyebrow. Chinese dragons' faces were much more expressive than that of the other dragons. "Would it be less uncomfortable to sit on the hard ground if you were a boy?"

Luke shook her head. "I shouldn't have said that. A girl is what I am, and I'm doing my best to live with what I got."

"But you look like a boy to me." Meiming cocked her head. Her steady gaze made Luke shiver, but not in the way she usually felt when someone paid her too much attention. "I will keep referring to you in the male, if you don't mind."

A sudden warmth rushed Luke's body and he had to swallow tears. No statement had ever made him feel this good. Maybe it was finally okay to see himself as male, if only when he was with Meiming. "I'd be delighted." He got up and bowed before settling on Meiming's tail. "I hate this body, but adapting it is very complicated for humans, involves dangerous surgeries, and isn't always satisfactory."

"Unfortunately it's nothing I can adjust with my magic, I'm afraid." Meiming looked apologetic, and again a shiver of warmth spread through Luke.

He wasn't used to so much attention, so he tried to change the subject. "What about you? How does a Chinese dragon get to America without knowing what she is?"

"Oh, that's a long story." Meiming turned her face away and stared at the wall. "It'd bore you to death."

"I don't think so. You're a fascinating and very beautiful creature. Why would I be bored by your story?" Luke's heart shivered a little. Since when was he so open? He had learned to guard his heart well, and now he was laying it at the feet of a dragon.

"Thank you for being polite."

"This is a truth chamber," he reminded her. "I cannot be polite if it goes against the truth."

Her head whipped around. "That's true, isn't it?"

"Of course it is. We have no choice." Luke smirked at the visible surprise on Meiming's dragon face. "I am really interested on how you came to be here in America, and not in China with the other Chinese dragons."

"Mom came here before I was born." Meiming stopped. "I should probably start at the very beginning." She sighed deeply.

It was clear to Luke that there was a lot of pain tied to the subject, so he shook his head. "Just start wherever you feel comfortable."

"Mom never told me much about her time in China. It must have been difficult. What she did tell me, though, was that she had to flee to save her family when she was only fourteen. A cousin of hers was in danger of being executed during the Tian'anmen Square Massacre in nineteen eighty-nine, and my grandmother sacrificed her life to save his. Since the authorities were chasing down the whole family, Mom took them as far away as she could, using magic if she had to. She never said so, but I'm sure she was deeply in love with her cousin.

"When they arrived in America two years after their flight, they were separated. Since she wasn't of age then and her father and grandparents were deceased, she was put into foster care without any information of where the rest of her family was. It broke her heart. She's been looking for them for as long as I can remember." Meiming sighed, and Luke wanted to put out his hand to pat her. But he didn't. It was a sorrow he couldn't ease. "Mom never spoke of her first two foster families, but the last one seemed to have been okay. We visited them occasionally when I was still little. Since my father abandoned Mom after she got pregnant, she supported me all on her own. Too proud to contact the American dragons, she trained and worked as a secretary to support me.

"I loved our holidays. She always took me to a tiny lake in these mountains as far from civilization as she could get, and we would fly and swim and be happy together. That's how we met Telanuel one day.

"I think he fell in love with Mom because he came with us and courted her. They even got married and Telanuel became my legal guardian, although Mom probably only went along with that to get a form of security for me. One day when I returned home from school—I was barely ten—Telanuel was sitting on our porch with a hard face and tears in his eyes. All our things were packed, and he told me that Mom had died in a massive car crash on her way home from work. Many humans had been killed or injured, but Telanuel only cared for Mom's death. He bundled me up and took me to his house here in the mountains. We lived there without ever meeting anyone. Only when Mordekay fetched us to Hilldale did I see other people again. But I wasn't very popular, especially at Tangerine High. Without Telanuel, I'd have been lost." Meiming looked up. Her voice wobbled as she said, "He's like a father to me. I can't just abandon him. I know he's got a good heart. It just broke when we lost Mom."

Luke didn't know what to say. All of a sudden, Telanuel had become more than a name, more than one of the bad guys in a film. He understood Meiming's desire to help him, but knew that whatever she tried would be in vain. He stroked her tail and pondered what to tell her that might help. After a while he had an idea.

"My father always wanted a son." He spoke hesitantly. "I was a big disappointment. But he raised me as best he could and was surprised that I managed all the things he'd planned to teach his son. Of course I did. I was eager to please him. A smile from him meant the world to me. He turned me into a dragon hunter, gave me all the tools I'd need, and planted a seed of hate by making dragons look like evil and dangerous animals. As much as I mourned his death, I was proud to take over his responsibilities." He considered his next words carefully. "When I found out that dragons were intelligent creatures and could turn into humans, an emotional earthquake shook my world. I felt as if I were a murderer, not the knight in dented but shiny armor that I'd thought I was. Could Pa have been wrong? But then, Mordekay confirmed my father's words and I was glad I got back my peace of mind."

"But he was lying." The tip of Meiming's tongue touched his cheek for a tiny moment and it comforted him more than he was ready to admit.

"Not really. He just strengthened my prejudices and used my perceptions without correcting them. That's not literal lying."

"For me, that's even worse." Meiming huffed. "It's lying by telling a partial truth. I never cared much for Mordekay."

"Well, the point I was trying to make is that my whole life seems wasted, now that I know what dragons truly are like. I can no longer fight dragons the way I'm supposed to. I'd truly be a murderer then." Luke stared at his fingers. "But I still love Pa. He only taught me what he thought I'd need. If he'd known better, things might've been different. For him. And for me."

Meiming breathed deeply, and silence fell; not the uncomfortable silence between people who weren't on talking terms, but the comfortable space people needed to think. Together they waited.

THIRD CHAPTER

*N*icole groaned when White Crow insisted for the umpteenth time that they couldn't start a fire despite the wood pile ready in the open fire place of the sitting room. She was cold, and the house was big, old, and drafty. Also her fingers itched. Sitting on the faded sofa in the darkened room where the furniture was barely more than shapes in the dark was so boring, she could fall asleep. She needed something to do, and Lydia wasn't back yet. How were they supposed to discuss battle plans if she didn't come?

Herbert smiled at her. "So you've got bumble-bees up your bottom?"

"Sorry?"

"Oh, that's an old saying from my ancestors' home country." He grinned even wider, displaying a still impressive array of gleaming white teeth. "It means you're fidgety. Would you like to come with me?"

So Nicole followed the small pink dragon to a room at the back of the ground floor. As he opened the door and turned on the electrical light, her eyes widened. Big bookshelves lined the windowless walls from the ground to the ceiling that was two stories high. Each shelf held so many books and scrolls that they seemed to bend under the weight.

"The Royals' private library." Herbert chuckled as Nicole stepped forward with wide eyes and trembling hands. So. Many. Books. She could barely wait to get started on them.

"Are there many about witches?" she asked.

"I haven't the slightest idea. The king always meant to catalog the whole collection, but he never had the time to do so." Herbert settled on a longish seat padded with dark red leather clearly designed for a much bigger dragon. His legs dangled in the air but he didn't seem to mind. "Sit down, girl. You're making me nervous."

Obediently Nicole sank into the only human-shaped chair. "How does one get the books from the top shelves?" she asked. "There are no ladders."

"They're not needed." Herbert mumbled something, and a book came floating from the far side of the room. "That's an easy spell to learn," he said as he caught the book with his left paw. "But to do so, you'll have to learn Dragonish, the language of the dragons first. And that's the tricky part."

"But I don't want to learn magic." Nicole shivered at the thought of how difficult it had been to make her erratic gift do what she wanted it to do. It would be so much easier to simply forget about her strange talent and live the life she'd lived before. She thought about all the books she'd given away and moaned. It'd cost a fortune to replace them all.

Herbert interrupted her thoughts by pressing the slim volume that he'd fetched with magic into her hand. "Read this," he ordered, and his tone didn't leave her much choice although he did not use the Commanding Voice.

Nicole complied reluctantly, and only because she'd come to like the old dragon. The booklet was only a few pages long but little black scratches filled the margins that didn't look one bit like writing but obviously were. She marveled at the delicacy of the strange script. How could a dragon write so small? But then she remembered that they could turn into humans. Still, the writing looked elegant and beautiful. It beckoned her, and a part of her heart longed to learn the script.

With a stern call to herself, she pulled her gaze away from the foreign script and concentrated on the main text. It was written in plain English and seemed to be a report of some sort.

She read the first entry that told about a case of spontaneous human combustion. An elderly man had burned to death when he visited the toilet of a cheap restaurant. The report's author proved that the case could be explained with the man's excessive drinking and smoking habits.

The next few articles were about spontaneous human combustion too, but the burnt people were all female and middle-aged or older. For all these cases the report's author couldn't prove external ignition without a doubt, but thought it likely since most of the victims were alcoholics and smokers. The final three cases, one from Scotland, one from Texas and one from India, concerned young women in their mid-teens. Every single one of them seemed to have gone up in flame without anything nearby that would explain their demise. In that section, a lot of the strange black symbols filled the margins, as if the commentator had added plenty of thoughts about these cases.

The report's author insisted that the cases in Texas and Scotland were genuine. The one in India might have been an honor killing since the girl had been a Muslim, not a Buddhist.

Still, he couldn't rule out that she'd been one of the few cases that really did go up in flames without outside triggers.

And that's where the booklet ended. It had no final conclusion or any other 'this is the end of the book' line that fiction or non-fiction usually had. The report's author simply stopped after delivering the facts without ever thinking about what they meant.

Nicole let the booklet sink and looked at Herbert, folding one leg over the other. The seat was incredibly comfortable. She could read here forever. But why this booklet? It seemed completely unrelated to any of their problems, but she was sure the old dragon had a good reason for making her read it. "What's this got to do with humans and dragons?"

"Nothing." Herbert sat up with his front paws on the dragon seat and his hind legs dangling down, watching her without blinking. "It's got to do with you. Did you understand the last three cases?"

"The young girls?"

Herbert's gaze was unwavering. "They were witches like you."

Nicole's jaw dropped. "How can you know? Why didn't the report's author explain…" Well, no, a normal human would scoff at the idea of a teenage witch. "Why? Why did they burn up?"

"We've sent specially trained dragons to investigate each death and they confirmed that the girls were witches." Herbert still looked at her steadily. "However, they did not know what they were and had no training whatsoever."

"So they caught on fire because they accidentally used a spell?" Nicole's fingers grew cold.

"It's more complicated than that. What do you know about magic?" Herbert resembled the statue of a teacher—a dragon teacher.

"I can use a few spells, that's all." Nicole leaned back and made herself comfortable. This seemed to be a longer conversation than she had anticipated.

"I thought so." Herbert sank back down on his padded bench and let his forelegs dangle like his hind legs. He breathed deeply and explained. "Magic grows in every sentient creature on Earth. Normally, it simply dissipates and the people are none the wiser for it. In some creatures, magic pools up in differing amounts. Unicorns and dragons have a lot of magic, werewolves grow very little and use it up once a month. There are a few more creatures in small, magically screened pockets of the world, but most have moved to other worlds when humans began to invade every corner of the world."

"Are we that horrible?" Nicole knew how badly humans, as a species, treated Earth, but hearing it from the mouth of someone unrelated drove a spike of guilt through her.

"*Ignorant* would be the better word." Herbert smiled. "My point is that every sentient creature, humans too, grow magic, mostly without knowing it. Dragons instinctively gather their magic before it can dissipate and use it to stay hidden or to shift. The royal family saves their magic in the realm of Queen's Magic where it stays on even after their death. Queen's Magic is a place but also isn't. It's hard to explain, especially if one doesn't have access. But queens can go there, so if you want to know more about that, you'll have to talk to Lydia."

"Lydia isn't queen, and as far as I know she'll never become queen if that means leaving Colin." At least that was something Nicole was sure about. "And anyway, what does all of that have to do with burning teenies?" Being flippant about those gruesome deaths seemed to make them easier to bear.

"You are growing magic too, my dear. A lot of it. And like all witches, you pool it inside of you instinctively." Herbert's gaze caught hers and she noticed the deep concern on his surprisingly expressive dragon face. "In witches—and that's what you are, whether you like it or not—magic gets stronger the longer it isn't used. You've been without training for what … sixteen, seventeen years?"

"I've been using a lot of it lately." Nicole hated how defensive she sounded.

"That's a drop on a hot stone, my dear." He sighed. "You'll have to use a lot more magic than you've used so far, and you need training so you can determine how much magic has accumulated."

Nicole didn't know what to say. Where would she get the necessary training? She didn't know anyone using magic aside from the dragons, and if she talked about that to her parents, they'd consider her crazy.

Herbert wasn't done yet. "Our big problem is that there's no witch anywhere that we know of who could teach you. It seems that there aren't any left, or they're hiding so well that even we can't find them." His smile was wary. "So all we can offer you is the training a dragonet would get. And I don't know if that'll be enough."

Nicole's mouth grew dry as he continued.

"The minute your magic reaches a critical level, you'll catch fire and burn up just like those girls did. You're practically a walking bomb, my dear."

I didn't really want to take Colin to the throne room—all those dragons dead set against our love must be intimidating—but

I didn't have a choice. As I had learned the hard way, dragons weren't really capable of finding compromises. If the Chinese had some sort of interim leader, as I suspected—they wouldn't have presented us with a declaration of war otherwise—my dragons urgently needed one too. And since they wouldn't accept Colin as my soul mate, I'd have to choose one they would listen to instead.

Naturally that wouldn't be easy. I trusted Angie, and she was my mother's sister, but she had refused to become queen, and I didn't think I could change her mind now. The Head of Council wasn't a good choice either since she had no access to the realm of Queen's Magic. That left Meiming and me. I sighed.

The stony, windowless corridors seemed endless, and with every step the noise of talking dragons grew louder. Still, they never drowned out Colin's soft footsteps. I'd turned back into my dragon form, partially to impress the other dragons and partially to keep Colin sheltered behind me should we encounter a dragon as unyielding as the late librarian. When the tunnel finally widened to the waiting chamber in front of the throne room, I turned to my love and said, "Do we dare a clear declaration of our love? It might make things harder for us in the long run, but it'd at least be honest."

"I know how important honor is to dragons, so whatever you've planned, I'm in." Colin grinned up at me and my heart grew soft. How much I longed to nuzzle him, if only we had the time. Instead I helped him up on my neck, much higher than I normally would carry a rider. It was a little strenuous but I managed to lift my head high. As I opened the big double doors to the throne room and entered, carrying Colin at the dragons' eye level, the discussion slowly died from the doors to the dais. I fought a grin. We'd certainly captured their attention.

This time the vast cavern with the whitewashed walls was filled to the brim with dragons. My gaze flickered over all shades of scales: brown, red, blue, green, orange, gold and more. I nodded as friendly as I could to every dragon who made eye contact. The number of those who dared was surprisingly high, but I didn't know if it showed their defiance or partial acceptance. Right now, though, it didn't matter. All that mattered was that they seemed ready to listen to me.

On the dais, the Head of Council stood facing the Council and the throne room. Her tail swished from side to side, a clear sign of agitation. Before she could open her mouth to say something—most likely an accusation or some such—I stepped beside her and turned to the gathered dragons.

"I am here," I announced, secretly proud that Colin's head was slightly higher than that of the Head of Council. I'd estimated that well. "I am ready to take on the responsibility of a queen for the time being. I will not, however, concede to giving up my soul mate." A low grumble went through the hall, but I continued unperturbed. "The coming war will require us to act united, and it will require us to take human concerns into consideration too. If we cannot work out a solution, this war will be the end of our dragon community. Colin will tell you why, since he's the only one in this room who knows how the human leaders will react."

I noticed his surprise in a tightening of his legs around my neck, but he spoke loud and clear as if we'd discussed this before coming here. "Even if the Chinese dragons fly in over the north pole, they'll eventually be spotted by humans. The first sightings will be put off as unreliable or superstitious, especially since you'll use your magic to obscure and hide the truth. But when the fighting starts, you will need your magic and your strength elsewhere, which means that humans will discover what you are and where you are. When photos and videos of your ferocious fighting—and I'm assuming that it'll look impressive—show up on the internet, human leaders will classify you as a threat to humanity. They'll send in the military, and they'll kill you in great numbers." He proceeded to tell them about the kinds of weapons humans had developed, and I noticed the scales in many of the faces rise in horror. Colin finished with the words, "If bad comes to worst, I'll take Lydia in. She's been established as a human already and therefore should be able to live as one. But the majority of you will be wiped from the face of this Earth for good."

FOURTH CHAPTER

"Liar!" The Head of Council glared at him.

"We can all go to the truth chamber, and I will repeat my words. You know it works on humans too." Of course Colin had the right—the only—answer to her challenge, but I feared for a second that the Head of Council would bite off his head.

Instead she lowered her gaze. "What do you suggest?"

Colin shrugged. "I am not qualified to tell dragons what to do. But I do know that Lydia is. I am sure she has some excellent advice." His voice sounded much more friendly than I'd expected, given the animosity of the dragons.

The dragons murmured again, but this time it sounded more confused than angry. Were they surprised that he hadn't come up with plans for them? Could their refusal of having a human queen consort be based on the fear of being ruled by someone they considered inferior? Well, that needed investigating at some point, but right now I had more important things to do. First, I had to do something about the Chinese. "We'll need scouts to scan the skies for the approach of the Chinese dragons. If they want to wage war on us, they've got to come here, and a flight of dragons should be hard to overlook even if they use magic to conceal themselves against human eyes. Any volunteers?"

There were enough younger dragons who were eager for action, but only two older dragons. I gave them the command and impressed the need upon them to remain unseen. "Stay under cover at all times. We'll only have the advantage of surprise if they don't know that we know when and from where they're coming."

The youngsters moaned but the grown-up dragons nodded their approval. Fine. That was settled, so now I could take Colin to my parents' house.

Just as I meant to turn away from the gathered dragons, he spoke up, just loud enough that I could hear him. "Don't forget that we'll have to go back to school or our parents will get frantic."

If he went, I would go with him, and that was something the dragons wouldn't enjoy at all. *Drat!* With a sigh I said, "While we're at it, I have to go back to the humans. I'm safer there."

"But we need your guidance and counsel," one of the council-members said, and I realized that Telanuel had left a big hole in dragon society.

"We need a new Head of Security," I said. When I informed the dragons about Telanuel's actions and Mordekay's plans, they growled, appalled. I turned to the Council. "I consider kidnapping a potential queen and trying to enslave all of dragondom high treason. Don't you agree?"

"Death to the traitors," they shouted in unison, and the dragons present cheered.

"I think we'll keep the final verdict for when we have them in our grasp—if we can capture them at all. I'm quite sure that we'll see more of them." It wasn't a pleasant thought, but one that needed to be spoken. I breathed deeply until the throne room fell silent again. "My suggestion would be to have a human and a dragon as a security team. Our friends from the tribe that took us in when we were in need so long ago have always been faithful and trustworthy. Therefore I suggest Angela Cordelia Draconia Dragonis and White Crow—"

Loud clamoring broke out. "He's dead!" "Wasn't he killed?" "How come he's alive?" sounded through the hall.

I called them to reason and explained with a few words that White Crow had gone into hiding to protect me from Mordekay. I also reminded them how much Angie had suffered when she'd thought him dead. "Therefore I suggest Angie and White Crow as the new Head of Security team. Any objections?" I used a tone that made it clear that objections weren't truly welcome, and was glad when no one spoke up. I didn't really have any arguments as to why they should take over security aside from feeling safe whenever I was with either one of them. Hopefully that was enough.

It seemed to work. After a short discussion, the Council approved my suggestion.

"But we won't let you go back to the humans again," the Head of Council said, a defiant glint in her eyes.

I sighed and addressed her underlying worry as directly as I could. I remembered Father's advice that directness was always best with dragons. "Mordekay and Telanuel want to keep dragons a secret, so they won't dare to attack me when I'm in the middle of a human crowd. I wouldn't be half as safe if I stayed here. And anyway, you can always phone or text me at any time. I'll keep my mobile active and will check it regularly."

"Mobile?"

"Text?"

The question marks on their faces were telling. I needed a go-between … Longbow! He was just the man I needed.

"Longbow has proven to be trustworthy. Also, he has a mobile and knows how to handle it. Therefore I will leave my contact data with him. He will be your man if you need to contact me."

To demonstrate my words, I pulled out my mobile and called Angie. She answered at the third ring.

"Hi Angie." My greeting stopped her from telling me anything about the others. "Can you come here immediately and bring White Crow and Longbow?" For some strange reason, I suddenly remembered the librarian who had died trying to murder me, and an idea came to me. "And bring Herbert if he's still with you."

"Sure. We'll leave right away." That was something I'd always admired about Angie. She picked up subtext in everything I said and acted without many words. She'd make a splendid Head of Security. I ended the call and turned back to the assembled dragons.

"I also noticed that the Royal Library is no longer cared for." Appointing Herbert, who seemed well liked in the community, to an office would probably take the dragons' minds off Angie's and White Crow's qualifications. Also, it'd give Nicole access to all the books she could ever need. I continued to speak with a smile on my face. "Therefore I appoint Herbert as interim librarian." I stopped, not knowing the rest of Herbert's dragon name. Instantly the dragons clapped their approval. Herbert must be considered suitable.

I looked around the throne room. Despite joy about Herbert's assignment, every single dragon looked tense. A little diversion was called for; after all, it'd take the Chinese dragons quite a while to fly here all the way from China, especially since they had to hide from the humans. So I came up with another plan, one that might loosen up the dragons a little.

"I suggest we celebrate the promotions of Angie, White Crow, Longbow, and Herbert. I think we all need a little feast right now."

"Why don't you take the Royal Vow first?" The Head of Council looked at me expectantly. "*That* would be something to celebrate."

"Not as long as you don't accept Colin." My answer was steadfast, and I ignored the frown on her face as I called for food and music.

Colin marveled at how competently Lydia handled the dragons. She truly was a born ruler. If only there were a way she could be queen without giving up her heart. He sighed. Maybe Nicole had enough magic to turn him into a dragon. That'd solve the problems, wouldn't it? He'd have to ask her. But first, he'd call Harm to make sure Nicole was safe.

Sitting on Lydia's neck he could see the whole giant cavern that the dragons used as their throne room. The light brown walls had been smoothed and rounded like most of the rooms in the castle, and pillars of stalactites grown together with their stalagmites stood in irregular intervals. Harm answered on the third ring.

After they'd exchanged the usual greetings, Colin said, "If you're wondering, Lydia promoted Angie, White Crow, Herbert, and Longbow. That's why they had to come. Now I need *you* to take special care of Nicole."

"As if I'd take my eyes off her." Harm chuckled and Colin relaxed. Nicole would be in good hands.

"And don't allow her to do *too* much magic." Hopefully his sister would listen to reason.

"Herbert's working on that." Harm changed the subject rather abruptly, as if he wasn't entirely comfortable thinking about Nicole's magic. "Did you imply that Lydia told the dragons what to do?"

Colin grinned. "She took control and the other dragons are delighted."

"She agreed to become queen?" Even through the tinny speaker of his mobile, the surprise in Harm's voice was clear.

"No. She's their interim leader."

"Clever." Harm spoke to someone away from the phone, so Colin looked around some more. He watched dragons and Native Americans decorate the room with greenery. They were way too silent for a celebration. "I think they're still very worried about you," he whispered to Lydia, not wanting to admit that he felt the same.

"I know. That's why I ordered a feast."

Just at that moment, Harm's voice sounded from the mobile. "A party? Oh man, do I feel left out." But his tone made it clear that he was quite happy to be with Nicole.

Lydia addressed him directly. "When will Angie and the others be here?"

"They left five minutes ago."

"Great. Time to get the dragons to loosen up a bit." Lydia giggled. The sound was so unusual in a dragon that many of the attendees looked in their direction.

Colin ended his call, then asked, "How much longer do I have to sit up here?"

"Oops, sorry." Lydia helped him down by lifting her front leg. When he reached the ground, she shifted and led him to the back where a couple of chairs had been put up for the leaders of the tribe of humans to participate in the festivities. Some drummers were setting up their instruments and an elderly lady in a leather dress with long, gray hair tied into a loose braid smiled at them.

"Good thought," she said to Lydia. "We haven't had a real celebration for years."

Lydia smiled and the two talked a little. Watching them, Colin could tell that Lydia liked the protectors of the dragons. Hadn't she said something about a special bond she'd felt when she first landed in front of the castle? What if that bond was stronger than her love for him? What if his love wasn't strong enough? He sighed. Why did life have to be so complicated?

"Colin, may I present to you the Guardians' Warrior Chief?" Lydia pushed a man forward with bare shoulders so wide, Colin could barely look past them at her beloved face. The chief's leather trousers groaned when he moved due to his impressive leg muscles. When Lydia continued talking, her voice sounded worried. "I thought he could teach you how to fight just in case you're faced with a bad situation."

"He won't have much time," he reminded her. "School starts in a couple of days."

"I know, but still…" Her voice trailed off. Obviously the threat of the Chinese dragons and Mordekay's escape worried her more that she wanted to admit.

His heart went out to her. Whatever would come, he'd protect her with his life. So he smiled at the muscular man and said, "I'm ready whenever you are."

The Native American nodded and walked toward the exit door. Colin followed him without a glance back at the beginning of the festivities.

Time passed slowly for Meiming. The hoard in the little cave she was in was comfortable enough, especially since she'd never had one so big, but she longed to leave. Only her promise bound her … and the strange knight. How a man could be in a woman's body she didn't understand, but she knew it to be true. The chamber's magic pressed down on him just as much as on her.

Away from Telanuel for the first time, her thoughts wandered. Why hadn't he told her she was a Chinese dragon? If only her mother hadn't died so young. Maybe she could have told her more about her roots. Why hadn't Telanuel dispersed her feelings of being inadequate or even a freak? Not knowing why she was so different from other dragons had hurt so much. She gazed at Luke, who lay curled up on the gold with the tip of her tail as a cushion. This stranger accepted her just the way she was. Being her enemy hadn't stopped him from being friendly. Why wasn't Telanuel like that? Had she been wrong in trusting him? And what about Mordekay? She'd always known he was bad news, but what would he do now that she was no longer around?

A noise in the tunnel leading to the cave woke Luke. In an instant he stood facing the cave's entrance with his sword poised. When Lydia entered, he relaxed and put his jagged weapon away. He nodded at Lydia and smiled at Meiming. "I'll find us something to eat," he said and strode out of the room.

"A very considerate girl." Lydia watched him leave.

"He isn't a girl." Meiming wasn't sure if it was such a good idea to contradict Lydia, but the magic of the chamber wouldn't let her say anything else. "Inside he's more manly than most of the men I've known. Not that there were many…" She allowed herself to remember a few of the men Telanuel had brought home. Most of them had been polite to the point of being indecipherable, but a few had been thugs from the local neighborhood. Whenever they'd shown up, she'd hidden herself in her bedroom.

Lydia sat on the gold beside her. She didn't turn into a dragon. "You know, I'd meant to leave for my house to see how the others are faring, but some things interrupted my plans. So I thought I might as well spend some time with you to find out what I can about you.

You said your mother was buried, not burned. Was she human?"

"She was a dragon like me." Meiming let gold fall from her fingers. It clinked when it rejoined the hoard. "We just didn't have enough money for cremation. Pa said it didn't matter because he'd sung Mother the final rites already."

"Hmmm." Lydia stared at the ground in front of her. "I'll have to do some research on that. Didn't your mother tell you anything about royal magic?"

"No, but Mordekay talked about it sometimes," Meiming admitted. "But I never paid him much heed."

"Very wise." Lydia grinned, and suddenly Meiming wished they could be friends. She'd never had friends, since Telanuel had insisted on keeping her hidden aside from school.

"Fact is that you've been using Queen's Magic a lot. That indicates that you're of royal blood." Lydia's gaze transfixed Meiming. "However, there's no record of you being born or of you having married into any of the royal families I've researched. There are only very few royal families I can investigate. Especially the Chinese know nothing of you, although they did lose a princess a long time ago. Where did your ancestors come from?"

Meiming shrugged. Her roots weren't a secret. "My mother left China when she was fourteen because her mother was killed trying to protect a cousin. So the family had to flee. Mother worked here and fell in love with a human. He left her before I was born, and it nearly broke her, but she didn't give up. She raised me as best she could, and then we found Pa—I mean Telanuel. He was in love with Mother right from the first moment. I was still quite young then, but I could tell.

"Mother liked him. A lot. But she'd lost her heart to my father, and Telanuel knew that. There was a hurt in his eyes that never left. But he was good to us, and he loved me like his own daughter. I can't believe he..." Her voice trailed off.

Lydia didn't dig deeper. "What about your grandmother or your great-grandmother? How far back do you know your family's history?"

FIFTH CHAPTER

"*M*om told me a little of it." Meiming closed her eyes and recalled the old stories. "My great-grandmother lived in the northern provinces of China. She married late, after she'd given birth to my grandmother. That must have been when the Americas were at war with Europe. My great-grandmother died during a famine that killed many, many Chinese. Mom always said she starved to death to feed her child. My grandmother was the sole survivor of our family.

"Barely eighteen, she traveled southwards, always hoping to find a better life there. She barely dared to shift, stayed hidden most of the time, and had to fend for herself. Since so many other people had been as badly affected by the famine as she, there were hundreds of thousands of people looking for a new life. Of course there were some bad people too, so she had to use her magic occasionally, and not only to protect herself. That way she found friends, and they vowed to be a family. They stayed together and finally found work in Beijing. It was a hard life but one that gave my grandmother satisfaction.

"She even fell in love with the brother-in-law of one girl of her chosen family, and they got married. When my mom was born, my grandmother was in heaven. At least that was what Mom always told me she'd said. Family was most important to her, more important than anything else, and she protected hers fiercely.

"They had such a loving family even though they weren't really related. They weren't registered as family, and that's probably what saved her sisters and their husbands when my grandmother was killed."

Lydia's eyes grew wide. "She was killed?"

"There was a gathering of students on the Tian'anmen Square. They were demonstrating for improvements at university and of the Chinese political system. Soldiers were ordered to disperse the students, by force if necessary. The son of one of Grandma's adopted sisters was there, and when he fled, a group of soldiers followed him. Grandma managed to save him but was caught soon after. They shot her without a trial." Meiming blinked several times to suppress her tears. It had been so long ago, but it still hurt, even though she only knew her grandmother from her mother's tales. She swallowed the lump in her throat and continued. "Mom fled the country. That wasn't easy for a fourteen-year-old girl, but she did it. Later she told me whatever she remembered from Grandma's stories, and I soaked them up like a sponge." She looked at Lydia but the tears in her eyes blurred the image. "Mom might not have loved Telanuel the way he deserved, but we were happy until she died. I was as devastated as Pa, but we were there for each other. And then Mordekay showed up. I found him repulsive because he was too dark and moody for my liking, but he helped Pa."

"Oh." Lydia looked up with surprise. "You've got a color preference concerning dragons?"

"I wasn't talking about the color of his scales." Meiming shifted and sat beside Lydia. The gold clinked but she ignored the enticing sound. "Whenever people think, and they practically do that all the time even when sleeping, they emit a bright, colorful cloud, a little like a mist, that surrounds them. Thinking dark thoughts, being angry or unhappy, or feeling very sad darkens that cloud. Most people have some darkened patches in their mist. Pa's was always precariously balanced between light and darkness, and it often took me a lot of effort to cheer him up. Mordekay was the only person I ever met whose emissions were completely dark."

Meiming blushed at the admiration she saw on Lydia's face.

"I think the stuff you call mist is what humans call an aura. It would be interesting to see if all Chinese dragons can see it or just you." Lydia sighed. "If only the Chinese were coming for a friendly visit, not a war."

"A war?" Telanuel had allowed Meiming to watch human TV, so she had an inkling about how devastating a war between dragons could be. "Why would they come for a war?"

"Don't you know?" Lydia's eyebrows rose. "Telanuel sent an emissary in the name of my parents who poisoned the Chinese royal family. They're all dead. The war is the Chinese's reaction to that murder."

"Murder?" Meiming felt the blood drain from her face. Had she unknowingly been responsible for the death of dragons? Once Telanuel had brought a young man who'd been very reluctant in passing gifts to dragons. She'd forced him. Had Telanuel deceived her? Or had he been deceived by Mordekay?

Meiming's heart contracted so hard, she moaned. A gigantic boulder settled on her heart.

"I didn't mean … It wasn't … I…" Meiming hid her face in her hands. "Oh God … a whole family!"

"The royal family. And if you truly have royal blood, it was your own family he killed." Lydia's voice sounded tender.

With a river of tears barely held in check, Meiming kept her face covered. "You don't understand. I'm the murderess. I told the young man to give gifts to dragons although he didn't want to. I used my special voice on him until he finally obeyed."

"You didn't know." Lydia's hand touched Meiming's shoulder. "It's all been part of Mordekay's plan. You couldn't have known."

"I should have suspected." Meiming felt her voice quiver and shut up before she couldn't keep her tears back any longer.

Lydia stroked her back, not saying a word for a long time. Finally she whispered, "It's not your fault, Meiming."

Meiming barely heard her. It was as if the bleak time after her mother's death had returned. Her thoughts circled, screaming "freak" and "murderess" at her. She'd always knows she was defective, no good for anything. This proved it. She shivered, fighting tears. No, she wouldn't cry. Not in front of Lydia. If only Pa were here. He could … But then she remembered that he'd been part of the problem, according to Lydia. But what if Lydia was lying? No, that was impossible in this chamber. She must be telling the truth, and therefore Meiming was as surely a murderess as the poor man she'd forced to deliver the poison. It would be best to end it right here. If only she knew how. Maybe flight would get her captors to kill her.

Jumping up, she ran toward the cave's exit just as Luke returned. He dropped the tray he was carrying—cocoa spilled everywhere—and opened his arms. She stumbled right into his embrace. Hiccupping and crying, she tried to talk, but he just shushed her and stroked her back until her crying finally subsided.

"She feels guilty because Mordekay or Telanuel tricked her into ordering a human to take poison to the Chinese royals," Lydia explained. "I didn't mean to make her feel bad. I only wanted to get to know her better. Because if she truly is a descendant of the lost child of the Chinese royals, I wouldn't have to become queen."

The sorrow and guilt withdrew enough that Meiming could blink away the tears and turn. Still she clung to Luke. "You don't want to be queen? But isn't that what every dragon wants? I mean, Pa always said that becoming queen is the best thing that can happen to a dragon."

"I'd rather be with Colin." The words sounded heartfelt and tired, as if Lydia had been looking for a way out for an eternity. "But I'd understand if you don't particularly want the job either." Her glance wandered between Luke and Meiming.

Meiming blushed. A weight she'd never known existed lifted from her shoulders. She'd never liked Pa's plan of her becoming queen of the American dragons, but now that Lydia had admitted that the rank came with strings attached, she realized how much his pressure had burdened her. If only Pa hadn't made her turn an innocent man into a murderer.

Her emotions must have been clearly visible on her face because Lydia said, "I could take you into the Queen's realm. If you are who I think you are, you should be able to find your ancestors. It'd be a chance to admit your guilt and apologize."

"They're still alive?" Meiming frowned and let go of Luke, who began to clear up the mess the spilled cocoa had made.

"No, but a part of them is still there." Lydia pulled a face and got up. "It's hard to explain. Let me show you." She held out her hands.

Tentatively, Meiming took them, and was jerked out of her body. Alarmed, she tried to free her hands, but they seemed to have fused with Lydia's. She gazed around in growing panic. The world had turned gray. There was nothing familiar around her, only a pale yellow shimmer where the gold used to be.

"Don't be afraid," Lydia said. She resembled a human who'd put on a dragon's hide. Scales covered her from head to toe, but her physique was human. "You're not in danger."

But Meiming felt the grayness reaching for her, pulling at the barriers she'd put up when her mother had died; the barriers that kept the flood of unshed tears at bay. "I can't…" She ripped her hands from Lydia's grasp and stepped back.

To her great relief, she found herself in her body again. In this version of the world, the gold looked like gold, Luke was just getting up with a worried frown on his face, and Lydia was still holding her hands. Meiming sighed with relief.

"I'm sorry. I'm really sorry," she said, "but I just can't do this."

"I know, it's overwhelming." Lydia let go of her hands. "We'll try again some other time."

Colin stuck his head through the door. "Ah, there you are. The dragons are asking for you. They want to hear a final speech before we leave them."

Lydia groaned.

"And half of them want to accompany you to the humans just to make sure you arrive safely." Colin grinned. Was he amused by the panicked look on Lydia's face? "Luckily White Crow managed to talk them out of it."

"Thank God for that." Lydia relaxed visibly. "Keeping three dragons traveling with three humans invisible will be hard enough."

"Three humans?" Meiming asked.

"Three dragons?" Luke said.

Lydia laughed. "Harm and I will have to take Nicole and Colin home, and you as well, Luke. And I want Meiming to accompany us. I don't dare to leave her here. Who knows how many more traitors are hidden in our society?"

Luke's face brightened. "Can you arrange for her to be in my courses at school?"

Lydia smiled. "I'll do my best."

Meiming stood frozen. She ... back at Tangerine High? Without turning herself invisible during recess, she'd become the target of Isabella and her friends again. But if she used magic, Lydia would think she wanted to flee. How could she ever survive this dilemma?

Telanuel paced up and down in the living room of the tiny apartment he and Mordekay had rented in a hotel on one of Hilldale's side streets. It wasn't far from the school, which was essential, but he didn't much care for the worn carpets and the smell of cooked cabbage that permeated the whole building. *How much longer does it take to go to the airport and back?* he wondered. Mordekay should have been back half an hour ago.

He walked to the tiny, grimy window for the umpteenth time, not ready to admit, not even to himself, that he felt lonely without Meiming. Having left her in the clutches of those ... those ...*imbeciles* made him feel as if he'd betrayed her. If only she'd been born a princess. Then all this scheming wouldn't have been necessary.

The metal staircase outside the flat groaned and rattled, followed by footfalls loud enough to wake the dead. Telanuel stopped pacing and turned his back to the window, waiting.

"Welcome to our hideout, Your Highness." Mordekay swung the door open as if it were the portal to a palace. The dark-haired man with the impossibly old-fashioned Chinese dress—a sort of cape-like cloak with wide sleeves that hid his hands—gazed around without saying anything. He took in the faded flowery wallpaper, the threadbare, once-green carpet, the scraped cabinets and shabby, once-red plush sofa. His black eyes were quick to assess the room, something Telanuel admired immediately. Also, the man's silence was a boon.

"Please do come in." Mordekay practically shoved the Chinese ambassador over the threshold. The man frowned but continued walking until he stood right in front of Telanuel.

He bowed, the typical polite bow of an Asian dragon. "Am I right in assuming that you're the stepfather of Her Majesty?"

"I am." Telanuel bowed, making sure he didn't lower his shoulders farther than the ambassador had done. After all, he was the legal guardian of the Chinese princess—or more precisely, the guardian of the dragoness they would pass as the last descendant of the lost princess. Now all that remained to be done was to phrase things correctly. Chinese dragons could be sticklers for words. "Have you had a pleasant journey?"

"If you call sitting in a machine that stinks of diesel and rattles like a child's toy pleasant, then yes." The man smiled politely, an expression that never reached his eyes. They made small talk until Mordekay couldn't stand it any longer.

"Can't we cut to the important part?" Thankfully he interrupted Telanuel, not the ambassador. Still, the Chinese man looked shocked.

Telanuel hurried to smooth over Mordekay's faux pas. "Please excuse my friend's impatient outburst. He's not trained in diplomacy."

"I understand." The ambassador threw Mordekay a cold glare which the black dragon in his human form ignored completely. "If bluntness is what your companion prefers, I am able to reciprocate. Where is our princess?"

"She went for a walk with one of her companions." Telanuel bowed slightly forward and lowered his voice so the ambassador had to strain to understand. "We thought it better not to have her around while we discuss the difficult times we're facing. She's still so young, and we only found out recently who she is. She needs training, but as you can see, our means are limited."

"That they are." The ambassador walked to the sofa and sat down, perched on the very rim. "We do expect to meet her soon, though."

Sixth Chapter

*T*elanuel simply bowed. His guts suddenly felt as if he'd swallowed a stone. How to get Meiming back was something they could think about when the ambassador was gone. He pushed the sensation aside and asked, "Did you find our advice sensible?"

"Without a doubt." The words were accompanied by a curt nod. "Using human transportation wasn't very comfortable and giving up part of our hoards was a struggle, but it will give us an element of surprise. Surely the American dragons will expect us from the north."

"I am sure they will." Telanuel wondered if he should offer the ambassador something to drink, but thought better of it. "Mordekay and I have been busy too. Our technician finished his gadget, and it's ready to be used."

"Very good." The ambassador looked out of the window for a moment before continuing. "Since we didn't want to cause suspicion, my fellow fighters are coming in small groups. It will take a few more days for all to arrive, and then we'll need to regain our strength. The human way to travel is surprisingly exhausting."

"School starts again next week. Since that usurper is extremely fond of humans, I expect her to return to school." Mordekay let himself slump into the only comfy chair in the room and slung one leg over the other. "Imagine my big surprise when I saw this." He held up a newspaper. The headline read:

Finally! Start of Construction on the New Hospital Wing

"They say that the school will be performing for the occasion, and the country's governor will show up for the groundbreaking ceremony." He grinned, which reminded Telanuel of a shark he'd once eaten. "So we've got everyone in one place. If we use the gadget on the humans, they'll kill the usurper for us, and we have our foot in the door to the humans' president. The governor has direct access to him and can easily take us along."

The ambassador's lips turned into a pencil line. "We don't care what you do with the usurper. We only want our queen."

"And you will get her if you keep the American dragons from interfering. I always keep my bargains." Mordekay's gaze rested on the ambassador until the small man twitched. "I will even allow your queen to rule the American dragons. The unity will be good for the whole of dragonkind."

"We concur." The ambassador got up and bowed once more to Telanuel. He did not turn to Mordekay.

Telanuel bit back a grin. All of Mordekay's big plans hadn't brought him the recognition he so craved. "We are honored to have you on our side."

After an exchange of many more polite phrases, accompanied by many bows and backward shuffling, the ambassador finally left. Telanuel shot around and hissed at Mordekay. "And how, pray, will we get Meiming back? The whole plan hinges on her being with us."

"Oh, don't worry." Mordekay leaned back, pulling the shiny, black marble that he was always playing with from his pocket and throwing it from one hand into the other. "I've got an idea or two. Trust me."

The dragons clearly didn't like that Lydia was leaving again, even though Angie was at her side. She and White Crow had decided that she was the better bodyguard, while he would be more useful as tracker and strategist.

Luke sat on Meiming's back observing the crowd of dragons surrounding the castle's rocky forecourt that was normally used as a landing platform. There had to be hundreds, but no one spoke. The whole scene was eerily silent.

"You know in your heart that you'll have to be queen someday soon," the Head of Council whispered to Lydia, but due to the silence, everyone heard. Luke noticed a lot of heads nodding.

"I've bonded with a human. As long as you don't accept Colin, you're out of luck." Lydia held her head high and flexed her wings. Colin was nestled right between them.

To Meiming's right stood Harm, waiting for Nicole to be ready to leave. Herbert kept whispering in her ear. Luke heard words like *training, scrolls,* and *prepare.* Obviously Nicole had been busy gathering information on how to use her strange abilities.

Luke still didn't fully understand what was going on with her. Still, he liked her uncomplicated way. She'd only smiled when Lydia had announced that they were to treat Luke as a boy. He still felt a pleasurable shiver running down his spine when he thought about that little speech. If only it were as easy to change the body. He sighed. Well, as soon as they were back home, he'd find himself a psychiatrist to work with. The hardest bit would be to make his aunt understand. The teasing and nagging at school couldn't become worse anyway.

Lydia took off and all the dragons' heads swiveled to follow her ascent. Luke grabbed the fringe of blue-green hair on Meiming's neck as the Chinese dragon rose too. Her flight was less powerful but far more graceful than Lydia's. Luke marveled at how effortless Meiming seemed to swim through the air. She was the most beautiful dragon he'd ever encountered. Warmth flooded him when he pondered that she was his friend now.

Lydia swerved back and fell in right beside Meiming. "Angie and I decided it'd be best if you'd live with us. That way I can help you whenever you need it."

"You said I'd have to go to school." Meiming's voice was low and timid.

"Aren't you at Tangerine High?"

"Since last year. Before that, I was homeschooled." Meiming stared down at the forested area they were flying over. Soon they would have to rise to use the clouds as cover. "They don't much like me there."

"They're just jealous because you're much more beautiful than any of them," Luke blurted out. He blushed when Colin gave him thumbs-up and grinned.

Meiming twisted her head to look at him. Her eyes were wide. "You really think that?"

Luke blushed even deeper. He put his left hand on his heart and said with exaggerated formality, "I swear you're the most beautiful girl *and* dragon I've ever had the pleasure to be acquainted with."

She laughed. It was a musical sound that made him want to hug her. "I'd say we're friends, don't you think?"

Luke's throat seemed too tight for air, so he simply nodded. Meiming winked and turned her head back in the direction they were flying. He watched the hairs on her sides flutter in the wind and tried to cope with his feelings. He'd always been fascinated by Meiming, even when he hadn't known she was a dragon. Some days he'd even daydreamed of being her friend, and on especially daring occasions, he'd dreamed of being her boyfriend. And now, one of his dreams had come true.

They flew the rest of the trip in silence. When they neared Angie's house, Lydia, Angie, Harm, and Nicole used their magic to keep their approach hidden. They landed in Angie's garden, and Luke noticed that except for Nicole, everyone looked rather strained.

"I'll make us a cocoa," Angie said and hurried into the kitchen. "Show Meiming the guest room, Lydia. As long as she's staying, it'll be hers. And you can use my computer and the credit card to order her some clothes, Nicole."

"That's going to be fun." Lydia grabbed Meiming's hand and dragged her along.

Laughing, everyone hurried inside after her. Only Luke stood there, feeling a little lost. After the camaraderie of the flight, the parting without so much as a farewell left him feeling cold. Despite the warm air of the spring night, he shivered.

"Why are you lingering?" Harm came back out and held the door open for Luke. "Don't you like cocoa?"

"I'm invited?" Luke's eyes widened. "But I'm … I'm a knight."

"Yeah, and Meiming is the Queen of China. So what?" Harm grinned. "Cocoa is for everyone, and the more so for our friends."

Luke's heart was close to bursting. This was the second person who considered him a friend, and again it was a dragon. *Oh boy, has Father been wrong,* he thought. With a smile on his face he entered Angie's cozy kitchen.

Half an hour and three mugs of cocoa later, he reluctantly called a cab and said his farewells. The others waved and kept talking, but Meiming followed him outside. No one seemed worried that she might flee, and Luke wondered about that. Did she really take the vow to stay that seriously? At the end of the driveway, she stopped.

"Luke." She stared at her feet. "Could I use your phone? Just for a short moment?"

"What for?"

"Pa'll worry." She looked up. "I just want to let him know that I'm fine."

Pondering, Luke looked at the brightly lit windows of Angie's house. They suggested warmth and illuminated the night, revealing a well-kept lawn and some rose bushes. The idea of letting Meiming phone Telanuel didn't sit right with him, but he also understood her. If it were his father, regardless how wrong he'd been, he wouldn't want him to worry either. With a heavy sigh, he pulled his phone from his pocket. "Promise me that you won't tell him where you are, and that you'll tell Lydia about this."

"I promise." Meiming wrapped her arms around him and kissed him on the cheek. "Thank you, Luke." Then she took the phone, dialed, and waited. Her face lit up when a voice came from the speaker. Luke couldn't understand what it said, but it seemed to make Meiming happy.

"Don't worry about me, Pa. I'm treated well. Everybody is nice to me." She moved the mobile to her other ear. "The reason

I'm calling is that the Chinese dragons have declared war, and it's our fault. Please face the Council and help me sort it out. We can still prevent the war." She listened intently and shook her head several times. Her expression darkened with every word Telanuel said. Finally she spoke again. "You're wrong. Murder has never been the right way to achieve one's goals, and *I'm* the one who's charged with it because I bespelled the poor human." Telanuel said something, but Meiming shook her head vigorously. "That is not something I want. It never was. *You* always wanted me to be queen. If you don't dissociate from Mordekay and turn up at the Council to admit to what you and he have done, I'll be your daughter no longer." Meiming's voice wobbled, and Luke's heart went out to her. "Please, Pa. See reason." She listenend. "But Pa…" Her voice broke and tears rolled over her face. "If that's how you want it, fare thee well." Crying silently, she pressed the phone to her chest.

Carefully—in case she didn't like it—Luke put an arm around her and pulled her against his shoulder. There wasn't much he could say, but she needed some comfort. "I'm sorry he didn't listen to you, but at least you're not alone. You've got friends now." He pointed to the house.

She looked up at him with her tear-stained face. "I know you are my friend. I'm not so sure about them."

"They trust you not to flee. No one's even spying on you." Why did her eyes have to be so dark? They were like two tiny lakes of night.

"I promised. And a dragon never breaks a promise." She began to worry her lower lip. "Only time will tell if they see me as a friend or as an enemy. And when the Chinese show up, I fear the answer will be clear."

Luke lifted her chin with his index finger and thumb. "You know something? I haven't known them for long, but so far, all of them have been extremely friendly to me. And as a knight, I used to be their sworn enemy. Now, I've got friends—for the first time in my life. I bet you'll be surprised if you allow them to see you the way you truly are: caring and protective."

She blinked away tears. "If they learn that I miss Pa terribly, they won't want anything to do with me."

"They'll realize that you won't let him pull you into something you don't want to be part of any longer."

"I'd still do my best to protect him from the other dragons' wrath." She leaned into him. "I love him too much to watch him get killed for the actions he took because Mordekay misled him."

"And that's why I love you so." He bent forward and ever so gently touched her lips with his. A tingling spread through his body, starting at his face. It felt as if he was on fire, but it didn't hurt. Meiming wrapped her arms around him and pressed herself close to him, seemingly enjoying the kiss.

After what seemed to be an eternity but couldn't have been more than a few minutes, a car honked. The taxi had arrived. Meiming withdrew. Luke didn't dare to look at her but his cheeks were burning. This was the best kiss he'd ever gotten.

"See you in school tomorrow." Meiming pressed the mobile into his hand. "Thank you for letting me use it, even if it was in vain." She turned and ran toward the house.

Luke didn't know what to say. His thoughts were revolving around a single fact: They'd kissed!

"Well, young man, I ain't got all night," the cab driver said, but there was a gentle chuckle in his voice.

Silently Luke waved to the house, entered the cab, and told the driver the address of his aunt's flat.

SEVENTH CHAPTER

When her mother woke her the next morning, Nicole groaned. School ... But then she remembered that Harm would be there, and Lydia, and Meiming, and she got dressed in a hurry. Despite the emptiness of her bookshelves and the rather babyish floral-patterned wallpaper in her room, she felt great. Today would be a good day. She felt it in her bones.

Herbert had promised to come to the forest in the afternoon for her training, and maybe she could even replace some of the books she'd so foolishly given away. Thankfully she'd kept her favorites till last, unable to part with them.

Colin peeked into her room. "How about we pick up Harm, Lydia, and Meiming on the way?"

"Great idea." She hurried through her morning routine and soon they were on their way.

"What about Luke?" she asked as they stopped at the curb in front of Lydia's home. "Shouldn't we pick him up too?"

"I don't know where he lives," Colin admitted. "We'll have to ask him. And four people in the back seat is going to be a tight fit, too."

They arrived at the school's parking lot with ten minutes to spare. Luke was already waiting for them—or more precisely, for Meiming. Both blushed when they saw each other, but held hands nonetheless. Nicole grinned and reached for Harm's arm.

When she looked up at him, the warmth in his eyes made her feel tingly all over. Was that her happiness at seeing Harm, or the first sign of bursting into flame? *I really, really need to get rid of my excess magic in a controlled way,* she thought. *It just won't do to accidentally blow up the love of my life.* Together they entered the school and sauntered toward their lockers when the voice of Director Miller-Fielding came from the loudspeaker system.

"If you've followed the news the last two weeks, you will know that a generous sponsor has ensured that the hospital can build and equip a new ward for children." The loudspeaker hissed and crackled, but the director's speech wasn't done yet. "Since the governor will be there for the groundbreaking ceremony next week, the school choir has been asked to sing a few songs. I also volunteered helpers who will take the guests to their appointed places and keep the premises clean. Since it'd be unfair if only a few of you would have to be there, I declare the attendance of the festivities obligatory. That means that everybody has to come, yes, you too, so don't ask for special permission. If you're not lying on your deathbed, you'll come. Oh, and to entice more volunteers, the school will pay for the buffet of those who actually help with the festivities. Welcome back to school, friends."

All around Nicole, teens moaned or sighed. Some slammed their lockers closed much louder than necessary, but she could only think how trivial those problems seemed compared to the threat of a war. With a sigh, she grabbed her math book and pencil case, kissed Harm on the cheek, and left for her first lesson.

Harm itched. The whole day in school he felt observed. He tried to catch whomever it was but always came up empty, no matter how fast he turned or how secretly he tried to spy with his mobile. By the end of the school day, he was so agitated that he actually jumped when Nicole put her hand on his shoulder.

"What's wrong?" she asked, and he told her about that strange feeling.

"You just need to get used to the crowds again." She nodded in the direction of Isabella and her cronies. "They still fancy you and try to undress you with their eyes. I'm sure that's why you feel watched."

Harm had to admit that she might be right. Isabella had been around a couple of times he'd tried to spy the culprit. He adjusted the lapels of his leather jacket. Maybe it was time to let it go.

Colin showed up with Lydia, Meiming, and Luke in tow. He wore a lopsided grin. "I'm annoyed by this groundbreaking ceremony. My course has been asked to hand out free sandwiches."

"Mine too," Nicole said. "I guess they want to make a good impression on the governor."

Luke snorted. "You're lucky. The theater group is in charge of making the sandwiches. I'll be stuck behind the scenes while you'll at least see the ceremony."

"You won't be alone." Meiming put her hand on his arm. "I volunteered to help."

"How about an ice cream?" Lydia asked. "We still need to figure out what to do about the Chinese, and how to stop Mordekay and Telanuel."

Harm licked his lips. Eating ice cream was his favorite pastime when he was living as a human, and his father surely wouldn't mind if he spent some time with his friends. Blackfeather was rather cool for a father.

"As much as I'd like to come, I need to practice," Nicole said. "But Harm can join you if he wants."

Harm's stomach dropped. No way would he leave her alone when she was struggling with magic. The time when she didn't believe was too fresh in his mind. "I'd rather stay with you." His hand slipped into hers. She beamed at him and that meant the world to him. He grinned. "We'll have some when we're home. A dragon will bring Father home this evening, and he's promised to buy some as a return feast." It still felt strange to call Blackfeather *father*, but the anger and the ball of ice he'd felt burdened with were gone.

Colin kissed Lydia on the cheek. "I'll take them to the forest and be with you in a heartbeat."

"Drive carefully." Lydia turned and walked with the others in the direction of the mall. Luckily it wasn't far, so Harm didn't worry about his friends.

The ride to the forest was too short for his liking. He would have preferred to remain cuddled to Nicole for much longer, but she insisted that she needed the training and he just couldn't bear the thought of leaving her alone.

So they marched through the woods to the clearing that was so familiar and held so many memories. Thankfully, Herbert was there already, and he'd brought a couple of things Lydia could use for her training. But first he handed her a heavy stone.

"You've read the theory. Now try to levitate this," he said.

"Why not something lighter, like a feather?" Nicole wanted to know.

"The lighter something is, the more precise your spell has to be or you'll incinerate the object or person in question." Herbert smiled. "And that's something we don't really want."

Nicole fidgeted with embarrassment, which made Harm consider her even more desirable than ever. As he found himself a fallen tree to sit on and wait, she looked into the sky and concentrated.

Meanwhile, Herbert unpacked a lunch big enough for a whole family. "Remember to use the sun for energy," he said as he piled donuts, cupcakes, sandwiches, sausages, fruit, boiled eggs and more on a blanket.

Nicole opened her mouth and swallowed as if she were drinking something. Then she tried again. The stone shot up like a rocket and grew smaller and smaller. She stared after it with her mouth hanging open. Then the stone became bigger again rapidly. Harm whistled. She was strong!

"I said levitate, not hurl." Herbert lifted his hands and the stone glided back into his backpack at a much-reduced speed. He scratched his chin. "Let's see. We'll need something heavier." He pointed to a boulder the size of a big dog. "How about that one?"

Nicole did her best and this time, the stone rose much slower. After the seventh attempt, she even managed to float it in place for a while. Herbert was as pleased as Harm. When Nicole juggled several heavy boulders at once, he fished the smaller stone back out of his pack again.

"Now make this as heavy as the boulder and float it," he said.

The boulders Nicole was juggling dropped to the ground with a thud, and she turned to the much smaller stone. Again and again, it shot into the sky and Herbert had to catch it. Again and again, Nicole tried.

Harm longed to kiss the frown off her face, but he'd only be in the way. And anyway, his neck tingled. Cautiously he gazed around as if admiring his surroundings, but he used that to examine the forest closely. Nothing. Just like in school.

"Look, I got it." Nicole beamed at him. The stone floated in front of her only supported by her magic.

"Well done. Now let's have a bite to eat." Herbert pointed to the feast.

"Oh, good. I'm starving." Nicole let the stone settle gently beside the boulders and hurried to the food. Harm smiled. Thankfully she wasn't one of those girls that always worried about their figure. He joined her, still bothered by the sensation of being watched. But try as he might, he couldn't see anyone anywhere close.

Chatting amiably, they ate. Harm wasn't very hungry so he left most to Nicole.

"You're still using too much of your own energy," Herbert said to her. "You need to power your spells with energy from the sun or you'll deplete yourself, and that's never a good idea."

"I'm trying, but it's harder than it looks." She pushed another donut into her mouth and spoke around it. "I finnit har do grasf fe differen befeen fe mafic and fe energy."

"I understand." Herbert fell silent and seemed to think. When Nicole had cleared the last paper plate, he spoke again. "Have you ever watched humans create energy with water? They store up a huge amount by blocking a river, and then they force it through thin tubes with some gadgets at the end. The water pours out harmlessly, and the gadgets make energy."

"Sure, I know how turbines work." She gathered the debris and stuffed it into Herbert's bag. Harm liked the fact she didn't want to leave anything behind.

"Magic is like the water. It would normally flow away. In your body and in those of dragons, the normal flow is blocked, so it pools. The spells we use are like the gadgets—how did you call them? Turbines? They use the magic to do whatever we want. However, to channel the water, I mean the magic, to the spells, you need energy. After all, there are no tubes for containing magic in your body. Holding magic and directing it into a spell comes naturally to most magic users, as far as I know. You just have to be careful about what kind of energy source you use."

"Oh, I see." Nicole yawned. "But filling myself with sunlight energy uses magic too that needs to be controlled by using my own energy, and that's why I'm still hungrier than I normally would be, right?"

"Clever girl." Herbert grinned. "But you should be able to replenish your body's energy with the energy you take in. It simply takes some training."

"In that case—" Nicole started to say when a short, stumpy bolt shot toward her.

Harm cried out and was on his feet in a heartbeat, but the bolt was faster.

Nicole's hands flew up, and power radiated from her. The bolt changed direction, shot into the ground, and dug itself in until the feathers at its end were barely visible. Fury blazed through Harm's body. He was at Nicole's side to catch her fall. More bolts rained down on them, and Nicole pushed outward with her magic. Harm could tell it cost her to keep them from hitting Herbert, him, or her, but at least she was drinking sunlight again after the initial shock. So he set her down gently and looked around for their attackers.

Eight sword-wielding men in tight black clothes hurried toward them under the bolts' cover. Harm roared, turned into a dragon, and spat fire. It felt good to release the angry heat he felt toward those attacking the love of his life.

The attackers shifted too. They were Chinese dragons, spitting streams of acid at him, at Nicole, and at Herbert. Magic blocked the yellow liquid and it hung in the air for a second before it dropped to the ground.

"Take us out of here," Nicole whispered.

"I'm stronger than they are." Harm readied himself to pounce. "And they can fly too."

"We need to leave now." She pointed to Herbert, who was sitting on the ground, biting his lip and cradling his arm. A bolt stuck out of it. "And they won't follow. I'll take care of that."

Harm found it really hard to battle down the anger than burned in his veins, but he loved and trusted Nicole enough to follow her advice, so he helped Herbert climb on his back and picked up Nicole with his front paws while she maintained a shield that kept the attackers from coming any closer. As he took off, she shot a blast of magic at them.

Immediately, they staggered and sank to the ground. Their legs looked strangely stiff. As much as they wriggled their long, sinuous bodies, their feet no longer moved. Harm pumped his wings to fly higher. Some crossbow-carrying Chinese stepped from the underbrush. One or two hurried to the stranded dragons, the others shifted and took off. They too sank to the ground with stiff legs a few heartbeats later.

Nicole giggled. "I made their legs as heavy as the boulders like I did with the stone. That'll keep them busy for a while."

Despite his pain, Herbert guffawed. "You're a marvelous foe, Nicole. I'm glad you're on our side."

Harm didn't say anything. He needed all of his strength to reach Angie's house with two passengers.

When they finally reached Angie, Herbert was burning hot. Still, he didn't complain. Harm shifted back into human form and led him inside, for once neither feeling sorry about the transformation nor worried that someone might see them. He was sure that Nicole was taking care of that.

"What happened?" Angie hurried toward them with a bag of medicines in hand. She indicated to Harm that she wanted Herbert on the sofa in the living room, so he stepped through the open door into the room with the beige walls, the wooden furniture, and the green carpet.

Herbert lay down on the sofa, closing his eyes and breathing hard. "I've been poisoned," he said to Angie, panting heavily. "Don't bother … with an old dragon … like me. Take … me home … where I can … die in peace."

His arm looked raw and sizzled when Angie put a cooling kit on it. "Thankfully it's not Dragon Bane," she said to Nicole. "Fetch Meiming. Maybe she knows what it is."

EIGHTH CHAPTER

A few minutes later, Meiming hurried into the living room with Lydia on her heels. Harm stepped closer to the wall to be out of the way. With six people, the room was clearly overcrowded.

Humming softly, Meiming examined the wound. "I know that poison. Do you have ginger? It's the only antidote that might help." Even from his place near the wall, Harm could see that her expression was lacking confidence. Still, Lydia hurried to the kitchen to fetch the ginger.

"We'll use healing magic and ground ginger," Meiming said. "But he'll most likely need much more magic than I can provide."

"I won't let him die." Nicole's eyes were hard as stone. "Show me what to do."

"Careful, little witch. You've … used up so much energy already." Herbert smiled at her. "I'm an old, old dragon … and when my … time's up, … it's up."

Nicole pressed her lips together and nudged Meiming. "Show me."

When Lydia returned with the ginger, Meiming had already explained the basics of dragonish healing magic to Nicole. They were standing side by side next to the sofa with their fingertips resting on Herbert's arm. The old man had lost consciousness, and Nicole's face was very pale.

A pang of jealously shot through Harm's heart, but he pushed it aside. Nicole would worry like this about every one of their friends.

Meiming sprinkled a little bit of ginger onto the wound, and Herbert gasped even though he wasn't conscious. The Chinese girl looked worried. "It's already spread farther than I thought."

"Let's get going then. What are you waiting for?" Nicole grabbed her hand and pressed it on the ginger in the wound, covering it with her own. As they worked their magic, a slightly orange-tinged cloud surrounded their hands. Nicole looked fierce—Harm felt proud to have won the love of a fighter like her—and Meiming seemed very surprised.

Soon Herbert's breathing improved and he relaxed visibly. Meiming withdrew her hand.

Nicole frowned. "Why are we stopping? We've only got half of the poison out."

"I know." Meiming sat on the ground, breathing hard. "But I'm getting tired, and this is delicate work. If I guide your strength wrong, I'll cause more harm than good." She leaned her back against the sofa and closed her eyes. "Let me rest a while. He already has a much higher chance of survival thanks to you."

Nicole yawned and sank to the ground beside her, also leaning her back against the sofa. "But I won't let him die!"

"Point taken." Meiming yawned too. Shortly after they were both asleep.

Angie waved Lydia and Harm out of the room. "I'll wake them in a quarter of an hour so they can keep going, but I think it best of you'd stay out of the way."

"We'll make some cocoa," Lydia said. Obviously, cocoa wasn't just Harm's go-to remedy. She pointed to the entrance door. "Colin and Luke will be here any moment, and they'll surely need some too."

Harm smiled inwardly. It was good to know that cocoa existed. Still, he paced up and down the kitchen and worried that Nicole in her stubbornness would overdo it. Finally Lydia had enough.

"Sit down!" She used a touch of her Commanding Voice and Harm found himself seated before he realized what she'd done.

"Hey, does one treat friends like this?" But he didn't get back up because she placed a cup of cocoa in front of him, and he had to admit to himself that the drink was a great comforter.

The door opened and Luke and Colin came in. Lydia equipped them with cocoa too while Harm filled them in on what had happened.

"Maybe you should train us all, Luke." Colin sat in the chair opposite Harm. "Thanks to your training and that I got from the dragons' protectors, I'm already feeling a lot less clumsy in my efforts of self-defense."

"That's a good idea," Harm said. "And we'd have to learn more about Chinese poisons. I'm sure there are some antidotes we need to have that are hard to get."

Discussing battle plans and training units, they covered up how worried they were. Finally Meiming and Nicole shuffled into the room and downed a cup of cocoa each with but a few gulps.

"Gosh, that was good." Nicole set her mug down. At Harm's questioning glance, she said, "We got the poison out, so he'll live. But we'll have to let the wound close on its own for now. If we try magic on it, it might infect."

The tension in the room evaporated, and soon the friends were merrily discussing school schedules to see where they could insert some training sessions in chivalric fighting.

As Meiming helped Herbert to heal, she felt something she never had before in her entire life. She felt at home. Using the kind of magic she was best at made her feel needed and useful, and the easy camaraderie made her forget that she was de facto a prisoner. Even school became fun because Isabella and her clique no longer dared to target her. Every morning, she woke up with a smile on her face. *If only this time would never end,* she thought.

Herbert's wound only needed three days to heal completely, but it took the old dragon another week to regain his strength. For the whole time, the friends trained with Luke and researched Chinese poisons with Herbert.

Meiming didn't much care for the fighting, and it became apparent that she wasn't very good at it, but she joined in nonetheless. After all, it allowed her to be close to Luke. Thinking of him always made her smile, and being with him ignited a tiny fire in her chest that warmed her through and through. Who would have thought that she'd ever fall in love with a dragon hunter?

One afternoon, her class ended early. With a smile on her face she left school, took off her schoolbag, and sat on a bench in the school yard to wait for their secret training session to start. She preferred the fresh air to the stifling corridors of the school.

Although it was raining gently, it was a wonderful day. The air was warm enough that she didn't need a winter jacket, and the rain washed away the dirt. Everything smelled fresh and ready to bloom. She closed her eyes and breathed deeply.

When she opened them again, a piece of paper floated in front of her face. It wasn't much bigger than the palm of her hand, but the photo on it drained the happiness from the day.

Mordekay held a knife to Luke's throat. The knight was lying unconscious on a plain concrete floor. For a second Meiming feared him dead, but then she realized that one didn't threaten a corpse with a knife. *He's still alive …* A tiny flicker of hope rushed through her. She reached out, plucked the photo from the air, and stuffed it into her schoolbag. Then she straightened and looked around the yard. Someone in a dark cape was approaching her from the parking lot. He was still too far away to recognize but she knew it would be Telanuel. With a quick kick of her right heel, she shoved her bag under the bench she'd been sitting on and stood up. Hopefully Telanuel wouldn't notice her leaving it behind for Harm or Lydia to find—for surely they would think she'd fled if she didn't show up for their training. Then they'd start looking for her.

To keep him from seeing the bag, she walked in his direction.

"So you've decided to come after all." His voice was as deep and warm as ever, and for a short moment, Meiming longed to throw herself into his arms. Why couldn't it be like it used to be? Why did he have to change like this? When her mother was still alive, he had cared about her and her mother, not about politics.

"Isn't there a way back to how it once was?" Meiming looked at him with tears in her eyes. "You used to be my father, and I love you enough to have met you anywhere. Do you really have to threaten people I like?"

He frowned. "I don't know what you're talking about. I've come to take you to an important meeting. We talked about that before your capture. To tell the truth, I'm surprised that no one is watching you."

"I swore I wouldn't flee." She didn't need to say more. Keeping one's oath had always been one of his very own maxims.

"In that case, consider yourself kidnapped." He bowed and swept his arm in an arc toward a waiting taxi.

"Will you release Luke if I come?" Meiming searched his face for the compassion that used to be there.

"If that meeting goes as we discussed, I'll do whatever you want me to do except turn myself in." His words were honest, if evasive. The mist around his body, although much dimmer than before her mother's death, didn't flicker or grow even darker.

Knowing Telanuel wouldn't say more, Meiming jutted out her chin, walked to the taxi, and sat in the backseat.

Telanuel slipped in beside her and patted her knee. "You'll see, it's all for the best."

"I told you that I'm not interested in becoming the queen of all dragons." She tried to sound as cold as possible and was quite pleased with the result. "I'm not working with murderers."

"Murderers?" Telanuel's eyes widened. "I haven't murdered anyone. I swear by your mother's soul."

A white-hot surge of anger welled through her. How dare he drag her mother into this? She balled her hands into fists, breathed in and out evenly, and fought down her wrath. "You told me to order a human with my special voice so he would give a special gift to a white dragon."

"I had to." He took her hand and smiled apologetically. "Try to understand. He was the ambassador the other dragons planned to send to China, and he refused to take my gift along."

She glared at him. "I still don't get it. Why did you have to send Dragon Bane to the Chinese Queen?"

His eyes grew wide. "But I never…" He swallowed and stared at his hands. "So they're all dead?"

"The whole royal family." For some strange reason, Meiming noticed the chemical scent of the taxi's synthetic leather seats right now. The silence seemed to stretch into eternity.

"He lied." Telanuel's voice was a low whisper she barely heard. "He openly lied to me. I thought that was impossible for dragons." He looked up at her. "The cocoa I sent was meant to contain a spell that would send them to sleep for several months. We were sure that the remaining dragons would embrace your return more easily if the queen and her children were knocked out. After all, you're not truly the missing princess, and the queen would have known right away."

Meiming decided not to tell him of Lydia's conviction. "Are you trying to say that *Mordekay* peppered the cocoa with Dragon's Bane?" It would be just like him.

"I can't say for sure." The 'but' hung unspoken in the air between them as he stared into her face. "Do you believe me?"

Strangely enough, she did. And she still loved him. She decided to try him one more time. "Come with me to Lydia. She's competent and just, but with a human heart."

"There's no way I'll ever bow my head to a humanized dragon or to a dragon with a human consort." Telanuel's jaw muscles twitched as he pressed his teeth together.

Meiming put her hand on his arm. "Don't you see what Mordekay is doing to you? You used to like humans. Don't you remember?"

"We're there." He jerked himself free, and his aura darkened.

With rain in her heart, Meiming followed him out of the taxi into a narrow side street with overflowing dumpsters and a green door with flaking paint. She dared not cry. If the meeting with the Chinese didn't go like Telanuel had insisted so many times it should go, Luke would be in peril. And she'd do anything to save his life.

When I left the school with Colin at my side, an eerie sensation forced my gaze to one of the benches in the school yard. Something with a red and green pattern caught my attention. "Isn't that Meiming's backpack?" I hurried over and pulled it out from under the bench.

"Why would she leave it there?" Colin frowned, and the knot of worry in my stomach tightened. What if something had happened to her? I should never have left her alone. Surely I could have forced the teachers to let her take the same classes I took. Maybe there was a clue about what happened in the bag. Why else would she leave it here? With flying fingers I folded back the flap and pulled the zipper open. A photo tumbled out and fell to the ground. I bent down and picked it up.

It showed Mordekay holding a knife to Luke's throat. At that moment, Harm and Nicole came out of the school, heading toward us. They had Luke in tow.

"This must be a fake," I said to Colin, showing him the photo. "But poor Meiming didn't know. She was surely blackmailed into coming along because she likes Luke."

Colin managed a harsh-sounding laugh. "Likes? She adores the ground he walks on."

"What's wrong?" Harm asked, putting his arm protectively around Nicole's shoulders.

"Meiming's missing, most likely lured away with this." I showed them the photo.

"Mordekay," Nicole and Harm said simultaneously.

"I'll kill him. I really will." Luke stood there slightly bent forward, balancing on the balls of his feet. His left hand clenched around the ivory hilt of the dragon slayer's knife, for of course we'd given back his property once it was clear he wouldn't attack us with it. How he had smuggled it past the school guard's scrutiny was beyond me, though. The inset glass vial with the Dragon Bane gave me the shivers. It glittered slightly even though the sun was well hidden behind the clouds. Luke looked ready to storm a castle. "Let's go and find her."

I agreed with him but didn't think that running through town brandishing a poisoned knife would help right now. We needed to know more. I said so, and everybody agreed, mostly reluctantly. "Let's skip training and gather at my place. Maybe Angie has found something. She meant to search for Telanuel's and Mordekay's hideout. They have to be somewhere."

"With the preparations for the governor's arrival they will blend in easily," Harm said. "Even without using magic. No one will remember any of them."

"We'll see." I turned toward the parking lot. "At least it's better to think before one leaps."

NINTH CHAPTER

*T*en minutes later we were sitting around Angie's kitchen table with mugs of hot cocoa in our hands and the contents of Meiming's school bag on the table. Aside from the photo, there was no clue as to where she might be.

Angie set down her cup. "Are you sure she's been kidnapped and didn't go of her own free will? After all, she's been working with Mordekay and Telanuel the whole time."

I shook my head, trusting in the judgment I'd made after our talk in the truth chamber. "She was just loosening up a bit. I had the feeling she just started to enjoy our friendship."

"And anyway, the photo proves she didn't leave without force." Luke's hand clenched and unclenched on the table as if searching for his weapons. "And the only people with an interest in her are Telanuel and Mordekay."

"Why would they need her?" Nicole asked. "Neither of them seems the fatherly type."

"She's a white Chinese dragon who can use some sort of Queen's Magic." Colin spoke low and everybody listened intently. "Mordekay arranged for the Chinese royals to be murdered.

He also killed Lydia's parents and tried to do the same with Lydia. It's perfectly reasonable to assume that he instigated the war because he wants to rule all dragons with Meiming as his puppet queen."

"He also managed to get the machine I built," Luke threw in. "It amplifies the Commanding Voice. I think he not only wants to rule the dragons but also enslave all humans."

That made sense and chilled me to the marrow. We had to stop him. And fast. "Any ideas of where they might be? I mean tall, handsome, bearded Telanuel with stocky, balding Smolinsky should be easy to spot. After all, they're a most unlikely pair."

"I've asked around but only drawn blanks so far." Angie got up to fetch the jug with more cocoa. "One thing that's worrying me, though, is the increasing number of Chinese tourists in town. I've never seen so many. If I didn't know that dragons never, ever use their hoard to pay for anything and that most are generally not comfortable using human inventions, I'd say that the Chinese dragons are coming by plane rather than flying themselves."

"They could have used the Commanding Voice," Nicole said.

Harm shook his head. "If I remember my history correctly, the Chinese don't have a Commanding Voice. Only their royals can use it."

"That's right," Angie said with a nod. "For diplomatic reasons from eons ago, the knowledge of that spell has been limited to the queens and their daughters. No, if the Chinese dragons want to come by plane, they'd have to pay. I say it's a coincidence."

"I can't sit here just talking." Luke jumped to his feet. He nearly shouted. "We have to find…" He stopped mid-sentence and slapped his forehead. "My mobile. Colin, can you drive me home?"

Colin seemed to be just as confused as I was, since he asked, "Why do you need your phone? And why didn't you bring it to school?"

"I didn't leave it, but a few days ago, Meiming called Telanuel on it, and back home I've got some tracking equipment. I can call Telanuel's mobile without him noticing and find out where it is." He pulled on Colin's chair. "Come on, man. We've got a girl to save."

Suddenly I had a picture in my mind's eye. Luke, the dragon slayer, on a white steed hurrying to save a dragon. That turned all the human fairy tales I'd read during my recovery on their head. It was hard to keep a straight face. It was even harder to let Colin and Luke leave without coming along. The tiny flat he and his aunt lived in surely wouldn't hold all of us. I hadn't been there yet, but he'd told us a little about it.

So we stayed behind speculating on Mordekay's plans. The longer we had to wait, the harder it became not to fall into brooding. The machine Luke had invented worried me, as did the growing numbers of Chinese people in town. I didn't believe in coincidence, so they either were dragons or the Chinese had sent their human protectors to help with the fight. After all, Chinese dragons were widely accepted by the Chinese populace.

And anyway, I didn't want to fight other dragons. It seemed so pointless to try to kill each other when a single, reasonable discussion could solve the problems. But would the Chinese accept Meiming as queen, provided we could get her back alive? Or would I need more proof?

Aargh, there I was, thinking of her again. Try as I might, I didn't manage to consider other things for long. My thoughts always came back to the small Chinese dragon. I had to admit that I'd grown quite fond of her.

My mobile rang. I picked it up so fast, I nearly dropped it. "Yes?"

It was Colin. "Luke's traced Telanuel's mobile. It's in one of the shabbier motels in town. Do you have something to write with? We'll meet there in half an hour, okay?"

I grabbed paper and pen and scribbled down the address he gave me. Hopefully Telanuel's mobile was still with him, and Meiming too. Waving the slip of paper through the air, I called, "Let's go."

In only a few heartbeats, we all bundled into Angie's car. Hopefully three dragons, a witch in training, a dragon slayer, and a peaceful human would be enough to overwhelm two rogue dragons.

Nicole stood beside Harm in front of a building that looked as if it had been built with patterned toy building blocks. At some point, someone must have decided to paint the reddish-brown bricks yellow, but the paint was flaking and the faded blue canopy over the entrance drooped. Her heart beat frantically. Would they meet Mordekay and Telanuel here? Would this give them a chance to capture the two before the war came to pass? And if they did, would they be able to stop the Chinese in time? Her knees trembled when Lydia said, "Let's go inside."

Angie took the lead. After stepping through the revolving doors, she approached a desk with a bored-looking girl who was painting her fingernails. Nicole followed the example of the others who were spreading out through the lobby to making sure the culprits weren't anywhere near.

"I'm looking for two gentlemen," Angie said and described the two men.

Nicole snorted, wishing they really were 'gentle men.'

At first the girl didn't want to admit that they had rented a room, but after a small bribe, Angie got their room number.

"But they're not in right now," the girl said, pushing a piece of chewing gum into her mouth. "They left with two Asians a little while ago."

Nicole's heart fell, but she knew they wouldn't turn back without looking at the room first. To keep the girl from telling Telanuel or Mordekay about the visitors, Lydia ordered her to forget about them. Nicole felt the familiar tingle of her friend's magic. She marveled that she could tell the different magics apart already. She hadn't been training all that much yet. Lost in thought, she followed Angie and the others up the stairs. No one in the group had the patience to wait for the lift.

A scent of burnt sweets hung in the air when they reached the third floor. It got stronger and more revolting the closer they came to the room in question. Nicole's throat tightened. What had Mordekay done this time?

Without much ado, Harm shouldered the door and it popped open. He stepped aside and let Angie go in first. Luke ran after her, and the rest of the group followed as best they could. Inside the shutters were closed and the stench was nearly unbearable. It was as if someone had forgotten their barbecue. Colin and Lydia opened the windows and the shutters, and everyone gasped.

"Meiming!" Luke ran to the girl who was lying on the ground in her dragon form. Her tail was extended into the bathroom and the fringe of hair along her body had stopped moving. Although her eyes were open, she didn't seem to see the intruders. She was barely breathing.

Nicole's stomach plummeted, and she hurried to Angie's side. Maybe her strength would be needed. Lydia obviously had had the same thought. Side by side, they knelt.

Angie put her hands on the dimming scales and flinched. "She's burning up. We have to get the fever down. Luke, get a towel and drench it in cold water."

Obediently, Luke walked along Meiming's body into the bathroom. He swore, loud and obscene. Everybody rushed toward him, squeezing through the doorway.

Meiming's tail hung over the rim of the bathtub which was filled with cold water. It hissed and steam had filled the upper half of the tiny, white-tiled room.

Angie swore too. "Dragon Bane."

"But she hasn't swallowed it," Lydia said.

"No, but it'll kill her anyway." Angie turned back to the unconscious dragon's head. "All we can do is ease her pain."

Luke's face drained of color, and Nicole's heart went out to him. What would she feel like if Harm were dying? They couldn't give up. "Let's at least try." She took Lydia's hand and pulled her toward Angie. "The two of you know what needs to be done, and I've got a lot of power. There must be a way to stop the poison from spreading."

"I don't know how. No dragon has ever survived Dragon's Bane." Angie looked apologetic.

But Nicole wouldn't take a no for a no. "The she'll be the first." She knelt beside the big head again and placed her hands on the forehead. "Show me how healing works and I'll find a way."

Lydia waved Angie to Meiming's other side and sat down beside Nicole. "Even if she doesn't survive, it's worth a try.

With the Chinese attacking, she's too valuable an asset ... and I like her. Angie, you take care of the pain. I'll help Nicole."

She put her hands over Nicole's, and all of a sudden the young witch found herself in a white void.

"This is a world between magic and the world of royal magic that only dragons can access," Lydia said. "Meiming is the flickering beam of light there."

Nicole turned her attention away from the whiteness around her and concentrated on the sliver of light. The tip was already darkening. The longer she stared, the more it began to look like Meiming. "Fine," she said. "How would you normally proceed?"

"We would order her core to heal. It's not really difficult, except that every dragon protects their core viciously." Lydia pointed to where the light was brightest in Meiming's chest. "I'll keep her distracted. You have to go in and find the right command." She began to sing a soothing song.

Nicole felt herself relax. *I mustn't go to sleep,* she reminded herself. Instead she approached the white dragon and reached for the glowing core. Before her fingers touched it, she was sucked out of the white world.

She found herself in an equally white realm, only this time the whiteness came from a snowstorm. White flakes whirled all around her, and a strong wind buffeted her from all sides.

Meiming's face hung over her, many times bigger than it would normally be and with much longer teeth. But the dragon didn't snap. Instead it spoke. "What do you want?"

"You're dying." Nicole leaned her head back, feeling slightly worried that she was exposing her throat like this. "I've come to help."

"The Dragon Bane has already burned halfway through my scales. I can feel it coming closer." Meiming lowered her head somewhat. "Once it reaches my bloodstream, it'll be over."

"Well, then stop it from coming closer. Build more scales."

"It'll simply burn through them." There was no vigor in Meiming's voice. "Thank you for coming, but there's nothing you can do."

Nicole had an inspiration. "And what about Luke? If Telanuel and Mordekay succeed, he'll be one of the first to die. After all, he's the last dragon slayer, and they know it."

"Luke's here?" Meiming's head shot up and her eyes looked far more alert than before.

Yes, Nicole thought. *This is the right track.* "He's worried stiff. If you die, his world will crumble."

"I have to see him one final time." Meiming turned and slithered over the snow, through the howling wind.

Nicole followed her as best she could. "If you survive, you can see him all the time."

Meiming stopped and stared at Nicole once more. Her yellow, slitted eyes never blinked. "I'd love to, but what do you suggest I do to stop the Dragon Bane?"

After walking through so much snow, Nicole was cold and growing stiff. However, Meiming seemed unaffected. There must be a reason for that, and Nicole was beginning to hope. If only … "Say, are you by chance an ice dragon?"

"I would think so." Meiming nodded toward the snowy world around her. "Whenever I withdraw into myself, I end up in this snowstorm."

"Well then, use that snow and the ice. Dragon Bane clings to your tail and burns through your scales. Use the snow and ice to wash it off from the inside out." Nicole stared up at the dragon's face.

Surprise showed in Meiming's features. Then, she closed her eyes and concentrated. The wind that howled around them in ever-changing whirls turned and blew in one direction only, carrying snow and ice with it. It howled and the world grew whiter and whiter. Soon, Nicole could barely see Meiming's clawed foot anymore, and she was leaning against it.

She shivered. Her eyelids drooped and her teeth clattered. If only it were warmer.

"It's working!" The awe in Meiming's voice woke a seed of stubbornness in Nicole. She wouldn't die in a magical realm trying to rescue a dragon. What would Harm think? She huddled as close to Meiming's foot as she could, using it as a shield against the wind. Closing her eyes, she reached out to her friends outside the magical realm for warmth. There was Colin's and Lydia's love, hot like a furnace, but when she tried to leech a little, her magical grasp slipped off. She felt around for Harm. Surely his love would warm her, but she couldn't find him. Where was he?

There! An unexpected source of heat. It was Luke's love, just as hot as Lydia's and Colin's. Eagerly Nicole dragged some of the warmth toward her. When she pulled it into the magical realm, it attached itself to Meiming's foot like a bracelet, growing thicker and stronger with every one of Nicole's heartbeats. Luckily it radiated so much warmth that her frozen limbs slowly came back to life. First they tingled, then burned until the pain was hard to bear.

"The Dragon Bane is gone," Meiming announced. She hesitated and looked down at Nicole and at the glowing thread wrapped around her foreleg. "What did you do?"

"I'm not sure, but I needed the warmth." Nicole rubbed her hands together to ease the pain. "Luke was giving his so freely, it saved my life."

"You've got one too." Meiming pointed to Nicole's right hand where a slender band of glowing warmth circled her wrist. "I wonder what it'll do."

"I guess we'll find out at some point," Nicole grinned up. "But for now, you're safe, and that's something he probably doesn't mind paying for with a little warmth."

"Thank you for your help." Meiming lowered her head. "But now, leave my mind, please." She nudged Nicole, who felt herself catapulted back into her body.

TENTH CHAPTER

When she opened her eyes, she found herself in the same dingy hotel room she'd been in before. There was no sign of a glowing bracelet, but she could still feel its warmth.

Meiming moaned and opened her eyes. She blinked a couple of times and when she'd oriented herself, she shifted into human form. "Thank you so much for saving me." She hugged Lydia and Nicole at the same time. "Trying to pour the Dragon Bane into the sink was so silly of me."

After Luke had helped her to her feet, they learned that she'd tried to hinder Mordekay's plans by getting rid of the Dragon Bane he'd prepared. Unfortunately she'd spilled some onto herself. Before she'd fallen unconscious, she'd managed to turn on the shower, shift into her dragon form, and hang her tail into the tub.

Harm entered the room. "We should leave," he said. "Telanuel and Mordekay are approaching the hotel."

Nicole had an idea. "You go ahead. I'll create a decoy. It's something Herbert taught me a little while back, and it comes in useful. After all, we don't want them to know we've been here."

While the others left the suite to make room for her, she put her hand on the shabby sofa and concentrated. For the first time since she'd admitted to herself that she was indeed a witch, she noticed a strong pressure against her body. Little flames danced over her arms. Was that it? Would she catch fire now? No! She'd come too far and learned too much already to die now. With her thoughts she grabbed the fire and hurled it against the sofa. *Copy,* she ordered, and immediately a second sofa stood in the room. It had the same worn once-red plush as the original. Even the small cigarette scorch mark on the left armrest was there. She grinned.

"Help me. Hurry," she said to Harm. Together they pushed the new sofa to the place where Meiming had lain just a few moments ago.

Then, Nicole closed her eyes and tried to recall all the tiny details of Meiming's lifeless body—the dark splotches on her tail and how limp it had hung in the tub with the running water; the motionless hairs mingling with the carpet; the seemingly lifeless body with dulled scales; the unseeing eyes. When the picture was clear in her mind's eye, she pushed the new sofa into her vision with her magic, pulling energy from the concrete building as best she could. When she opened her eyes again, Meiming's carcass was lying in exactly the same position as its original had before.

Nicole shivered as she touched the lifeless flesh. It felt incredibly real. She didn't doubt for a heartbeat that Mordekay and Telanuel would fall for it. And as a nice side effect, the flames that had been dancing on her arms were gone and she could barely feel the pressure against her body. She should use her magic more often.

With growling stomach but grinning, she and Harm left the room. Luke had picked up Meiming and carried her. Harm took Nicole's arm. Only now did she realize how drained and tired she was.

Colin handed her a chocolate bar. "I thought you might need this."

"Thank you." She opened and bit into it, thinking that what she really needed was already at her side. When they heard voices on the staircase, they withdrew down another corridor until Telanuel and Mordekay had passed. Then they hurried to leave the hotel before their enemies noticed them.

"And I tell you, the ambassador was convinced." Pride filled Mordekay's chest. Against his expectations, that little snit had managed to convince the Chinese ambassador that she was a descendant of the missing royal heir. And with his other plans all running smoothly, he'd soon be the true king of dragonkind. Then he could finally get rid of that nerve-killing stickler for dragon law. He threw his black marble high up into the air and caught it again. How he longed to laugh.

"Can't you stop playing with that thing for once?" Telanuel snapped as they ascended the stairs to their room.

"That's my safe-all, my fallback plan." Mordekay grinned as he threw and caught the marble. Not that he needed it, but with it he'd be invincible. It would always allow him to get away for another plan, and he was good at coming up with plans. "If all comes to naught, it'll turn me invisible and untouchable until I'm safe. An ancestor got it from a witch whose life he once saved."

The scent of charred barbecue filled the corridor in front of their hotel room, growing stronger when Telanuel opened their door.

"Meiming!" The scream ripped Mordekay from his reverie, and his jaw dropped.

The white dragon lay on the ground of their hotel room, dead as a doornail, and that idiot Telanuel hadn't even closed the door. Instead he was hugging her face, crying like a baby. Mordekay took care of the door problem but ignored Telanuel's obvious pain. Then, he examined the corpse, walking around it and finally passing through the bathroom door.

"Oh no." He didn't bother to keep the annoyance from his voice. "She poured out the Dragon Bane. I guess she got some on her pretty tail. What a pity." Now he had to adjust his plans once again. Her death was a nuisance, but he already had ideas of how he could work around that. He put a hand on Telanuel's shoulder, forcing his voice to sound caring. "What a loss. Unfortunately she can't remain here like this. We need to take her into the forest and burn her properly tonight. You do still have her powers, don't you?"

Telanuel shuddered. Then he wiped off his tears and began to sing the Hymn of Passing. Mordekay rolled his eyes. What good did it do to follow the old ritual? Well, as long as it helped Telanuel cope, he'd bear it. But that stinking corpse had to be taken care of as soon as possible.

When we arrived at Angie's, it was already growing dark. Luke rang his aunt to tell her he'd been staying with us for a while longer, while the rest of us found seats in the living room.

"How did you manage to free Luke?" Meiming stared at us wide-eyed as she rested on the sofa. "I tried to find where Pa and Mordekay had hidden him and couldn't discover a trace of him."

"He'd never been captured," Colin said. "Remember when Luke kidnapped Nicole? They must have taken the photo when they'd tied him up in the barn."

Meiming's mouth formed an O but no sound came out. Then she swallowed and lowered her gaze. "I'm sorry for acting foolishly."

"There's no need to apologize," I said and took Colin's hand. "If they'd showed me a photo with Colin in that position, I'd have come too."

"Why did they need you?" Angie stood near the door with her arms folded over her chest. "Were you able to overhear any of their plans?"

"I had to play princess. Pa wanted me to convince an ambassador of the Chinese dragons that I truly was the descendant of their lost princess." Meiming laughed nervously. "I think I managed it because the ambassador bent to the ground when he left. I'm sure he doesn't do that for everyone."

Angie nodded. "Did he say anything that might tell us when they'll attack?"

"No, he only said that they'd be ready when I was." Meiming shrugged and smiled crookedly.

She looked so frightened that I reached out and put my hand on her arm. "You've done well, considering the circumstances."

Her face lit up. "Oh, and when I asked them about Luke for the hundredth time, Pa finally said I'd meet him at the groundbreaking ceremony. So I guess they're planning something there."

"Drat," Colin said. "I've completely forgotten about that. The football team has been selected as waiters. Harm and I won't be much help that day."

"Since we now know where they are, we should be able to catch them tonight or tomorrow. That'll take care of the problem." Angie relaxed. "I'll make us some cocoa now."

I was glad she was in charge. It had been a good decision to appoint her as Head of Security. She would call White Crow now, and together they would devise a plan on how to capture the two traitors.

When she'd left the room, Meiming turned to me. She whispered, "Before the ambassador came, Mordekay did some sort of ritual on me. It felt as if he pulled something from me, but I don't know what. I've checked and double-checked. I'm just the way I used to be before. What if he'd taken something I can't remember?"

"Angie will force him to give it back whatever it was." Colin patted her shoulder. I looked through the living room. Harm sat on a comfy chair with Nicole on his lap. Luke stood close to the door, as if ready to pounce on anyone who might dare to enter uninvited. I smiled.

This was as good a time as any to finally find out whether my suspicion was true or not. I turned to Meiming. "Nicole told me about that snowy area in your magical realm. Have you been there often?"

She shrugged. "I hide there when things get too complicated or too hard. I love the snow. A part of me feels very much at home there."

"Could you take me there?" I stared into her eyes and saw surprise and fear.

"I ... I don't know."

I held out a hand. "Let's try."

With the usual ripple, we left our bodies behind and entered the white nothingness of the magical realm. Meiming and I took on our natural shape. Side by side we moved through the realm of white nothingness. I let her lead. At first, she seemed unsure of where to go, but then she took a sharp turn. I followed her.

Just a few heartbeats later, we were surrounded by ice and snow revolving around us due to strong winds. Below us lay a mountain range, mostly hidden in the white whirling.

Here, Meiming was the most graceful dragon I'd ever seen, and that said quite something because even in our world she was so much more beautiful than any other dragon I'd seen. She glided through the whiteness like a skater over ice. Her long sinuous curves glittered in the air and merged with the snow until she was nearly invisible, and the fringe on her body danced with the snow like an independent creature. There was no doubt about it: Meiming was an ice dragon.

I tried to follow her deeper into the snowy realm, but soon she vanished from my sight completely. Also, the icy wind sucked my warmth from me, and the whirling of the snow made it hard to determine directions. I looked for a safe landing place and found a group of suitable boulders. I set down in their slipstream, balancing precariously on my tail for a moment. When I managed to gain a steady stance, two pairs of slitted eyes glared at me from a hollow between two boulders leaning against each other; dragons' eyes.

For a moment, time seemed to freeze. Other dragons? Here? How did they get here? Who were they? Countless questions whirled through my mind and it took me a while to realize my mouth was hanging open.

The eyes blinked and two female Chinese dragons—as white as Meiming but one with a green fringe, the other with a light purple one—slid half out of their hiding place.

"Who are you?" the seemingly older one asked.

"How did you get here?" The eyes of the second one narrowed. "I warn you, we're not alone."

"I'm with Meiming." I barely managed to speak, so great was my surprise.

"That's what the other one said too." The suspicious dragon unsheathed her claws.

I hadn't even known that Chinese dragons had retractable weapons. Ingenious! My awe didn't diminish, but I did find my voice. "I'm Meiming's friend and the current queen of the American dragons." Well, that was true enough at the moment, and I didn't want to bother them with details right now. "Meiming is the center of a plot by two very evil dragons."

"Mordekay." The older dragon hissed and the younger relaxed somewhat.

She retracted her razor-sharp claws and sighed. "He seemed such a friendly person when he came here."

That was another blow to my stomach. "Mordekay has been here? And he was *friendly*?" I couldn't believe it.

"Such a handsome dragon. If I were still alive, he'd have been my type of dragon." The older one sighed. "What a pity that he turned out to be such an unpleasant person."

"Wait, wait." I walked closer to the boulders because the wind was still showering me with ice crystals, and I was slowly getting very cold. "Can you please tell me what happened in the order it happened?"

"Sure." The two dragons made themselves comfortable on the snow and I found myself a boulder I could huddle behind.

Being out of the wind completely helped a lot, but just in case, I flamed the boulder until it gave off some heat. Then I settled down to listen to the two dragons' tale.

"When I was young," the older one began, "my family was dead set against me marrying a human. Since I was a princess, they thought they had the right to decide whom I was to marry. So I ran away."

"Wait a moment. You were the Chinese princess that got lost during a hunt?" I bent forward with big eyes and only leaned back when she nodded. I knew it! Keeping the smug grin off my face was hard, but I managed—hopefully.

"Except that I didn't get lost, I hid until the hunting party was gone. Afterward, I lived with the human man I'd bonded with." A melancholy smile mellowed her features and a tear rolled down her cheek. It dropped to the ground with a low ching.

Crystal tears … their bond must have been as strong as that between Colin and me. The thought of Colin made my heart grow wide with sympathy for the old dragon in front of me. I cocked my head and listened while she continued her tale.

Eleventh Chapter

"It was a wonderful time, although it wasn't always easy. The humans in that village were so very poor, and there were so many regulations keeping them from food, it was a shame. I did my best to help. Although none of the humans aside from my husband knew where I'd come from and what I was, I was well loved.

"Then my beloved daughter was born during a strong snowstorm, and when I returned with her, everyone cheered. They'd thought I'd died in the cold. But then, the big famine killed nearly the whole village, including my husband. I took my child—she was just a toddler back then—and wandered the country in search of food."

"She gave every morsel to me," the younger dragon said. "She wanted me to survive and faded away herself."

Meiming's great-grandmother shrugged and went on. "I finally found a family of a tribe that had sworn to protect dragons. They, too, had suffered from the great famine, but they took us in. Knowing my child was safe, I finally let go of a world I no longer cared for. But instead of joining my husband in the human kind of death, I ended up here." She indicated the area around her. "Not that I mind. This way I was able to watch over my child, my grandchild, and now over Meiming, my great-grandchild."

The younger dragon took over. "I traveled around a lot until I finally settled down with a young human in Beijing. We also had a daughter. I named her Son Ling but couldn't protect her for long. Humans killed me after I helped the son of a friend of mine. It was an ugly death. I don't know what this culture revolution did to our folk that they get scared by a dragon. Before, we were considered wise and helpful." She shook her head. "At least my friend's son sang the old rites for me so I met my mother again."

Fascinated by their history, I asked for details and she complied, telling me about her chosen family and the Tian'anmen massacre. Finally she sighed. "As fascinating as our life stories might be to you, I doubt you came here to listen to them. You seemed more interested in Mordekay. So let's get to that, shall we?" I nodded, and she continued. "When Son Ling came here—a friend of hers by the name of Telanuel sang her the passing rites—we were delighted. We felt the increase of power she brought, so we decided that one of us should try to find the connection to the Queen's Realm. We knew it had to be somewhere because there had always been a tiny trickle of Queen's Magic filling this realm during all those years. Being the youngest and slenderest, Son Ling set out. She hasn't returned yet. But some time later, another dragon showed up. I can't really say when because time is rather flexible in here. He clearly wasn't related to us and was most definitely alive. He called himself Mordekay and lulled us with his charm."

Meiming's great-grandmother smiled wistfully. "It was wonderful to finally have someone to talk to again. Meiming never notices us, regardless how much we try to make her see."

Her daughter snorted. "He misused our friendship and did this to us." She crawled completely out of the gap between the boulders. A green chain tied her wings to her body. Its other end was fastened to the boulder, leaving the dragon barely enough room to leave the cavity between the stones.

My jaw fell again. The massive chain seemed to be made of stone, and I wondered why she didn't simply break it.

The great-grandmother must have understood my expression because she said, "The chains are made from magical jade. They're unbreakable. It must have cost him tremendous amounts of magic to bring them here, but bring them he did." She left the cavity too and I saw a similar chain around her.

"How does one get them off?" I turned into my human form, surprised that that was possible in the realm of dragon magic, and touched the younger dragon's chain. It felt warm and smooth, like polished marble.

"The owner of the chain has to give permission." Both dragons sighed. "Maybe there are other ways, but we wouldn't know. We don't have access to a dragon library."

"I do. I'll find out if there's another way to free you," I said.

"But why would he do that? What does he get from it?" Surely Mordekay would never do anything without a gain.

The two dragons looked at each other. The tentacles beside their mouths drooped, and Meiming's great-grandmother said, "He can use our magic like his own now. We can no longer protect Meiming."

"If only we knew where Son Ling is." Meiming's grandmother laid her head on the ground and closed her eyes. "*She* would protect her daughter."

I felt their desperation and it hurt. Instinctively I said, "I'll find her."

Two heads shot up with surprise. "You will?"

All of a sudden I wasn't sure if that was such a good idea. After all, there was a war coming. There was also the groundbreaking ceremony for the new hospital wing. If I took too long, I'd get into trouble with my teachers, and Colin would worry if I didn't return to my body at the same time as Meiming. Still, I couldn't leave the two of them like this.

"I'll do my best," I promised. "But first, I'll have to talk to Meiming." I turned into a dragon again and took off.

The storm hadn't improved. If anything, it had become even worse. I was buffeted to and fro and my field of vision was tiny. There! I caught a glimpse of something white and blue curled around a boulder. "Meiming!"

I dove to the place where I thought I'd seen her. I'd been right. Her head moved from side to side and she was calling my name.

I landed beside her boulder and grinned. "I'm here. Guess who I found."

"Lydia." Her gaze went over me as if I wasn't there. "Lydia?"

I waved a wing in front of her eyes, but she didn't see me. What the ... what was going on? Why couldn't she see me? I narrowed my eyes and stared at her. Her outline flickered as if she wasn't fully here, and behind her, the storm condensed into a vortex of snow, hail, and wind. It reminded me of when I pulled the plug in Angie's bathtub and the water swirled out. Could it be? Tentatively I reached toward it with the tip of my wing. The vortex tugged at it. It was difficult to believe but someone or something was sucking Meiming's snowy world away and she didn't even seem to notice.

Closing my eyes to slits and hoping I wasn't doing something foolish, I pushed off and threw myself into the vortex, hugging my wings as close to my body as possible.

Telanuel leaned against the beige wall beside the wooden door to the corridor of the hospital. Sitting on an undersized chair made of metal and wood, Mordekay glared at him. "Don't be such a baby." He adjusted some of the dials on the machine the knight had invented. "You probably caught a cold, that's all."

"I don't think so." Telanuel sniffed for the umpteenth time, but the scents of the humans were still old or far away. If they were caught fiddling with the hospital's loudspeaker system, their plan might be jeopardized. He was meant to keep watch, but he felt too dizzy and his stomach knotted all the time. What had he done? Meiming was as good as his daughter. So why had he agreed to that ceremony? What if it had proved harmful for her? Was that even still relevant, now that she was dead? He tried to phrase his worry carefully. Mordekay wasn't someone to take criticism easily. "I think we shouldn't have done that ritual."

"Stop worrying. She's dead already." Mordekay pressed a couple of keys on the laptop they'd brought. "She'll no longer notice that we stole some of her magic." He stretched and began to pack the laptop into its bag. "Done. Now pull yourself together and check for humans."

Still feeling as if he'd swallowed a ball of ice, Telanuel turned and peeked through the door. He also sniffed, but the traces of human body odors were all half a day old. The corridor was as empty as it could get—no wonder, this late at night. "All's clear."

"Then let's go." Mordekay shouldered the backpack with the laptop and marched through the door, already playing with his black marble again as if he had no other care in the world.

Telanuel did his best to ignore the dizziness and the ball of ice in his stomach and followed him. Surely the feeling of remorse would leave when the humans were finally ready to greet their masters.

The vortex's suction whirled me around like a piece of paper in a tornado. My stomach complained until I reminded it that it wasn't even here. I was hurled along with snow and ice, but since everything was sucked in the same direction, I wasn't buffeted half as badly as before.

When the ride became less wild, I dared to open my eyes fully again. The blinding whiteness of Meiming's magical realm was slowly dimming. The longer I traveled, the darker it became.

And then, the suction stopped abruptly, hurling me against a solid wall I could feel but not see. What was that? Blinded by the sudden darkness, I turned into my human form and groped around. Everywhere my fingers touched numbing coldness, wet ice and snow.

But what was that? My fingertips had encountered something warm and scaly. Could that be dragon hide? Had I found Son Ling? Had she also traveled through the vortex? Or was this the thief of Meiming's magic?

"Hello?" I patted the scaly, warm skin. "Are you Meiming's mother?"

Two big, yellow eyes opened and stared at me. They glowed, which made it possible to see part of the dragon's face. It looked just like Meiming. I breathed deeply, only now noticing that I'd held my breath.

"Who are you?" The dragon's voice was clearly female, thus confirming my suspicion. I explained as best I could without mentioning that I was temporary queen.

"I didn't know Mei Ming had friends. That's good to hear." She pronounced the name of her daughter slightly differently, as if it consisted of two words, not one. Then she bent forward. "Do you have any suggestions on how to get out of here?"

"Not yet," I admitted. "I don't even know where we are." I looked around in concentration, but all I could see was darkness.

"We're in Telanuel's mind." Her eyes closed again. "The fool is draining Mei Ming's magic, and hasn't got a clue about the consequences."

"Telanuel?" I could barely believe it. Hadn't the two other dragons said they'd talked to Mordekay? Was *everyone* visiting Meiming's mind? "Are you sure?"

"He used a different name when he visited Mei Ming's realm, but I am sure. His love for me was palatable even though I kept hidden." She lifted her head and pointed into the dark at whatever had stopped my flight. "Feel this? It's a wall of unshed crystal tears. Impossible to break."

A one-sided bonding? Was that possible? I couldn't help myself. My heart went out to the green dragon. It must be terrible to be bonded to a dragon who didn't bond back.

"And before you judge me, I loved him well enough," Son Ling said. "I just couldn't bond. The love of my life, the man I'd bonded with, left me before my daughter was born. I nearly died from that pain. I know very well how Telanuel is feeling, but there isn't much I can do about it."

I walked closer to the wall. It was transparent. At its base, piles of snow were slowly melting. There was enough snow around us to fill a small lake.

Wait a moment …

Snow …

Water …

Tears …

I had an idea. I just needed more snow. Much more, and there was plenty in Meiming's realm! I turned to Son Ling and pointed to the snowbanks. "Can you melt this snow?"

She shook her massive head. "Sorry, dear, I am an ice dragon. I could multiply it, but I cannot melt it."

"But that's even better. Make as much snow as you can." I shifted back into dragon form and blew a flame on the snow, careful to only melt and not vaporize it. Son Ling watched me for a moment, then shrugged and began to hum. Snow drifted down on us, and it got more and more. I melted it as soon as it landed. After a while, the water level around us rose higher and higher. Soon I had to fly which wasn't easy since the room seemed to be restricted as if we were in a big cave, not in a person's mind. Also, the end of the vortex kept spewing ice crystals at my back.

Son Ling hovered beside me. She stared questioningly at the growing lake blow us. "What are you trying to achieve?"

Before I could answer, the wall of crystal tears broke. The unexpected pressure surge slammed into me and everything went dark.

When I came to, there was still snow falling around me, but the wind had stopped and there were no ice crystals either. The faces of three dragons hung over me. They seemed so big that I realized I must have shifted into my human form again. A smile crept over my face when I realized that my body obviously thought it the sturdier form.

Meiming's great-grandmother gifted me a toothy smile. "You did it! You brought back Son Ling. We're forever in your debt."

"No, you're not." I sat up and looked around for the vortex. If at all possible, I had to cut the connection between Meiming and Telanuel. It wouldn't do to leave him access to Meiming's magical realm, for Meiming was using Queen's Magic. We were lucky that her realm wasn't yet well connected to the main realm of Queen's Magic. It would be something we'd need to take care of as soon as the war was over. Until then, we had to protect her at all costs.

"If you're looking for Mei Ming, she's been gone a few minutes." Son Ling shifted into human form and sat down beside me. "Thank you for helping me find my way back."

"You're welcome." I stood up and looked at the snow-covered mountain peak. As cold as it was, I was surrounded by beauty. "Do you know if the connection to Telanuel broke when we were ejected from his mind?"

Son Ling shook her head. "It's still there, but it slowed to a trickle. I believe washing away his crystal tears might have woken his conscience. I think he'll have to sever the last thread himself."

That was what I had feared. In that case, there was only one thing left to do here. I turned to Meiming's great-grandmother. "Am I right in assuming that you were a Chinese princess?"

"Oh dear, that's been so long ago, and it never mattered much to me." She cocked her head and shrugged, which looked truly strange in a dragon. "All these stuffy officials and their rules. I hated it, but Mother wouldn't hear a word about me giving up my post as heiress. So when I fell in love with a simple farmer, I ran away."

"They've been missing you, you know." I grinned, for now it was proven that Meiming was without a doubt the last Chinese Royal of my time.

She had the decency to blush, which gave her scales a slight pinkish tone. Were they transparent? Why else could I see the blush? She shrugged once more. "You see, no one knew the passing rites when I died. That's why I couldn't connect with my relatives. It was quite lonely here until my daughter arrived." Her next smile held so much love, I felt like an intruder.

"Thank you for telling me." I got up and stretched. Time to leave.

TWELFTH CHAPTER

The firm softness of a sofa told Meiming she'd returned to the normal world. Warmth pulsed at her wrist, and for a short moment the memory of the bracelet connecting her to Nicole surfaced, but she pushed it aside. She had more important things to consider. She opened her eyes to a darkened living room and feared the worst. How could she have lost Lydia? Could it be that their magics weren't compatible? Hopefully her friend was already back in her body. She didn't know what Colin and Harm would do when Lydia remained lost somewhere in Meiming's mind. Her gaze wandered around the beige living room, and it took her a moment to remember that she was at Angie's now and no longer in the shabby hotel room.

Luke was sitting beside her, watching her. He smiled. "Thank God, you're back."

Meiming sat up, finding it hard to hide her worry. "How's Lydia?"

"Oh, she's still asleep." He pointed to Lydia's body curled up on the other half of the sofa. "Colin said you might both sleep for quite a while so they went for dinner."

"I lost her!" Meiming grabbed his shoulders and shook him. "I don't know what happened but there was this snowstorm. I've never had such a bad one in my life. And then she was gone. I searched and searched and searched, but I couldn't find her. Colin's going to kill me."

"No he's not." Nicole's voice came from one of the comfy chairs. "When it comes to the magical realms, Lydia knows what she's doing, and also she's strong enough to protect herself. She'll wake eventually."

Meiming understood the witch's trust, but still worry nibbled at her. What would Colin do if Lydia didn't wake soon? Tomorrow was the big day—the groundbreaking ceremony—and director Miller-Fielding would be quite annoyed if they didn't show up.

Before she could work up a frenzy, Luke took her hand. "Everything will be fine. Trust us."

To her great surprise, his reassurance calmed her. What kind of magic was he wielding? It didn't matter. He made her feel safe, and that was all she needed right now. "I much prefer your company to Father's," she said. "Especially since he no longer seems to care about me."

Lydia sat up. "It's like I thought. Meiming…" She looked around, and her eyebrows rose. "Where is everybody?"

"Dinner," Nicole said and set her book face down on a small table beside the comfy chair. "We've only been waiting for you."

Her last words were drowned out by the loud grumbling of Lydia's stomach.

"Great idea." Lydia stood up and walked toward the door. "Let's eat. I've got some great news."

When Luke returned home to the tiny flat he shared with his grandmother glowing from his love and the news, she was watching TV like always.

"Hi sweetie," she called. "I was in town today and brought you a gift. It's on your bed."

With a tired smile, Luke walked into the living room and kissed her wrinkly cheek even though he already knew what the gift would be. "Thank you, Gran."

He went to his room, and on the bed lay a pink, frilly dress. It clashed horribly with his chainmail armor, medieval weapons, and other stuff useful for a dragon slayer that were stored on shelves or hanging on the walls. A ball of pain congealed in Luke's throat. When would she accept him the way he was? He picked up the dress and stuffed it in a bag with other girl clothes. "And it's not even my size," he whispered to himself.

Blinking away tears, he went to bed. Some day she would no longer be able to stop him from changing. He'd already started looking for a doctor who could prescribe the necessary hormones. Unfortunately they would be costly. Soon, he'd leave school. He'd have to work hard to earn enough for the medication, the shrinks, and the operations he would need. Some day, he *would* be the man he'd always been inside.

His thoughts wandered to Meiming. It felt good to know what she didn't have the same preconceptions as his grandmother. But he also remembered Lydia's words. Meiming was the last Chinese royal. As soon as they'd managed to end the war, she'd leave the country to go with the Chinese. His chest constricted at the thought. China was terribly far away; he'd looked it up on the Internet. Although it was a country with a fascinating history, it wouldn't be easy to visit her there, even should he be able to earn enough money for the trip.

He sighed. Why did life have to be so complicated? Lost in thought, he rolled around in his bed, finding it hard to sleep.

The next morning he woke feeling as if he'd fought a major battle, and it took a cold shower to remind him that today was the day of the groundbreaking ceremony. If Meiming was right—and he was quite sure she was—Telanuel and Mordekay had something planned. He considered taking some of his weapons along—it wasn't easy to fight dragons without—but changed his mind when he realized that there would be very tight security. So he only took a pendant that looked like the claw of a tiger but was a concealed knife, and a box of earplugs. Those might come in handy should the rogue dragons intend to use his gadget.

He was barely dressed in time for Colin, who had taken to picking him up every morning.

"Bye, Grandma," he called into the living room where the TV was blaring again already. His grandmother didn't answer, so he peeked in.

She waved him away. "I'm fine, I'm fine, Theodore. I'll see you after school."

Theodore was his father's name, which meant it was going to be one of *those* days again. He kissed her cheek. "I'll tell Mrs. Hanlow to look in, shall I?" His grandmother's best friend would keep her occupied and stop her from wandering the streets until he returned. He sighed and left the room.

"Hurry up," Colin said. "Miller-Fielding doesn't like us to be late, and also, we need to find out where Mordekay and Telanuel are."

On the way to the groundbreaking ceremony, he called the neighbor, wishing he could afford to pay for constant care, but his grant and her tiny pension didn't allow for that.

At the building site, he took two pairs of earplugs out of his box—one for Meiming and one for himself—and handed the rest to Colin. "You'd better give these to the others. When I invented my machine, I made these. They'll cancel the gadget's effect."

"Wow, great." Colin slapped his shoulder and pocketed the little box. "I'll make sure everyone gets a pair." Just then, his teacher called and Colin left, waving back.

Luke smiled. It was good to have friends, even if some of them were dragons. He looked around until he found the members of the theater group and followed them to a big tent at the side. Since the ceremony wasn't due for another three hours, the huge lawn area was mostly empty. Only a handful of men in black dresses was walking around, examining everything. Most likely they were part of the security team. It was a pity that the sky was overcast. With sunshine and without Mordekay, this could have been fun.

At the entrance to the tent, everybody was searched. Since Luke had left most of his weapons at home, he didn't object. The tighter the security, the better. Thankfully the security team didn't discover the disguised ceramic blade. Obviously the tiger's claw he wore around his neck was inconspicuous enough.

Inside, the tent was filled with several rows of tables. The ones at the left-hand side of the entrance were completely empty, but the rows on the right were piled with loafs of bread and packets of butter, cheese, boiled eggs, lettuce, tomatoes, and the like. He also spotted several towers of serving plates and two big heaters. They stood at the far end blowing hot air. The tent's interior smelled delicious but also a little burnt.

Some of his coursemates were already busy preparing sandwiches, so Luke found himself a place beside Meiming.

She was spreading butter on slices of bread, humming to herself quietly. After a quick kiss on her cheek, he handed her one pair of his earplugs and explained what they were good for.

She beamed at him, and the adoration in her eyes made him feel dizzy.

"Ooh, look at the lovebird freaks." Isabella, who was slicing cucumbers at a nearby table, pulled up one side of her lips as if she were smelling something rotten. "Hopefully their children won't inherit their freakiness. Oops." She put a hand on her mouth. "I forgot. Two *girls* can't have children, now, can they?" Her cronies giggled.

Meiming stared at her trembling hands, but Luke only looked at Isabella wordlessly. After a while she began to squirm.

"Stop gawking." Her voice sounded shrill.

Luke smiled and spoke just low enough that no one aside from Isabella and her friends could hear it. "You can insult me any way you want, but leave Meiming in peace."

"You can't make us." Isabella's eyes narrowed. "Freak!"

"I doubt you'd still look beautiful if I shaved off your hair one night." Luke grinned, showing his teeth. "I'm pretty quiet and very good with security technology."

Isabella paled, and turned back to her slicing. Meiming's hand crept into Luke's and she squeezed gently. "I love you, Luke," she whispered. "Regardless of what the other dragons will think."

Warmth shot through him as if someone had turned up the heater and sat him right in front of it. "I love you too." With burning ears, he returned to the task at hand. But one nagging thought remained. Regardless of their feelings, if Meiming became the new queen of the Chinese dragons, she'd need someone at her side who could provide offspring. After all, she was the last one of her bloodline.

Dressed in a black coat, Telanuel stood behind the platform that had been prepared for the governor's speech. It stood only one foot higher than the ground and provided good access to a spade stuck in the ground. He had reassured the security men beside him that he was one of theirs by not commenting on the man's misconceptions. The near lie made his stomach revolt and bile rise in his throat. Ever since a few days ago, his thoughts and his emotions were battling.

His heart told him to leave, but he had to stay. Dragons would perish like his beloved Son Ling if he didn't. They needed human slaves, their prowess in medicine, and their ingenious inventions. It was the only way to ensure dragonkind would survive. As dubious as Mordekay was, he was the only one who understood.

One only had to look at the gadget he'd organized. That machine was incredible, intensifying a power that humans weren't even aware of. It'd been centuries since the last witches were burned. And that was another reason why he had to keep going. Humans tended to kill each other for silly reasons. They needed someone wiser than they to supervise them and tell them what to do, or they'd die out sooner or later too.

Telanuel swallowed the sour foam and concentrated on the crowd gathering in the meadow. Most had brought umbrellas, even though it wasn't raining yet. Dark clouds hung deep over the city, which worried him a little. What if Lydia's dragons had somehow found out Mordekay and he'd be here? They could hide easily in the low-hanging clouds. *Since no one could have told them about Mordekay's plan, it is impossible for the other dragons to sneak up on us,* he told himself, and concentrated on the crowd of humans again.

More and more people filled the space, reporters with microphones and TV cameras as well as dictation gadgets or old-fashioned pen and paper at the front. He had no doubt that Mordekay's plan would work. He felt Meiming's magic course through his veins. It was less than he'd hoped for, but enough to make this work. The magic had stopped building up the same day his emotions had first overwhelmed him, but after spending three hours crying, he'd caught himself. Luckily Mordekay hadn't witnessed his breakdown. Telanuel had burnt the crystals he'd cried before the black dragon returned.

He pulled his thoughts back to the situation at hand. With his thoughts focused on the people in front of him, he adjusted his headset—another one of humanity's great inventions. Imagine being able to talk over long distances without magic.

"Stop fidgeting!" Mordekay's order sounded right in his ear. "The other guards will get suspicious if you can't stand as still as they do."

Telanuel knew he was right, but it was hard. He forced himself to focus on the mayor and the director of the hospital who had arrived to the applause of the crowd. Pretending to himself that he truly was a security guard helped. The school choir began to sing, and Telanuel relaxed. He knew the ceremony's timetable. The choir's song was the first step to his success.

While the speakers delivered their speeches, he scanned the crowd. Since the school had decided to get involved, it was most likely that Lydia and her clique were around. It'd probably be a good idea to spot them before they found him. There … wasn't that Harm carrying a plate with sandwiches, the traitor? Well, if everything went as planned—and they'd made sure that it would—the teenager dragons and their humans wouldn't be a problem much longer.

"When do we start?" he whispered into his headset.

"The governor has just arrived at rear of the hospital." Mordekay sounded calm and in control. "When he's finished talking, the gadget will have gathered enough power."

With bated breath, Telanuel waited for the crucial moment. The governor walked out of the hospital's main entrance door, shielded by four bodyguards. His portly figure with the balding head and the pudgy face remained unseen by the crowd until he drew close enough. Under the crowd's applause, he stepped onto the dais.

Telanuel didn't listen to his babbling. Instead he searched for Lydia. Where Harm was, his friends were usually nearby. And sure enough, Lydia was a little more to the side, handing out sandwiches to small children and their mothers. How fortunate. It meant that he could achieve two goals with one action. He grinned to himself.

A jerk went through his body like it had done the times he'd trained with the gadget. He pulled up the thin, scarf-like microphone he'd been hiding under the collar of his shirt, and stepped onto the dais. "Stop moving around," he ordered and everyone within hearing range froze on the spot. They seemed to take his orders quite literally. How convenient. A pang of sorrow shot through his heart and nearly made him stumble. How could he…? *This is important,* he called himself to reason. When he reached the main microphone, he called out to the crowd. "I am your king. Kneel!" And they all fell to their knees: men, women, the young, the elderly, even the toddlers.

It works! Why then didn't he feel happy? He shook his head. Time for part two. He took the kneeling governor's arm. "Stand up. You'll take us, my friend and me, along. And then we'll visit the President of humans in America."

"Certainly, Your Majesty." The governor got up and bowed, face slack and eyes dull.

THIRTEENTH CHAPTER

*A*gain a pang of sadness shot through Telanuel's heart. Although the people around him didn't seem in pain, they also didn't look as if being commanded was fine with them.

He shook his head; he had a task at hand.

"Stop it right there!" Lydia's voice cut through him like a knife and he stopped involuntarily. "You will come with me and answer to the community."

Her magic rippled over his skin and he felt the urge to comply, but Mordekay screamed in his ear. "Take the governor and get out of there. They're coming!"

Telanuel snapped awake and noticed Harm, Nicole, and the knight hurry toward them. None of them was armed—if one didn't count a tiny blade barely longer than his small finger—but together they would still be able to overwhelm him. He grabbed the governor's elbow and dragged him along.

"Come with me. Your life is in danger," he ordered. Suddenly the governor walked faster than he did. Part of him longed to turn and find Meiming, for surely she'd come with her friends. But then he remembered.

Meiming was dead. She'd died in great pain when she'd poured out the Dragon Bane. He'd told Mordekay countless times not to leave it lying around, and now it had taken Meiming's life. A sob escaped his chest. Meiming. The last connection he'd still had to Son Ling.

Tears flowed over his face. He tried to wipe them away but his hand only got tangled in his headset. He ripped it off and ran faster, crying more and more. Blinded, he ran toward the hospital, letting go of the governor, who slowed down immediately. He tore through the building like a madman. Humans shot out of his way as fast as they could. The only security officer who tried to stop him flew through the air from the impact as Telanuel rammed his shoulder into the man's stomach.

When he shot though the main entrance on the other side of the building, Mordekay was waiting for him in a human's car. It was dark green and rather plain, which suited Telanuel just fine.

"Idiot!" Mordekay said. "Get in."

Telanuel obeyed, and Mordekay took off with squealing tires.

"What a disaster," he said. "Well, at least it showed us that the gadget is quite efficient." His eyes narrowed. "Which can't be said about you. What's wrong?"

There wasn't an ounce of caring in his voice, but still it made Telanuel feel better. He tried to explain. "I'm missing Meiming."

"She's dead and burned. You sang her the rites. That's all you can do." He snarled at the other cars. "You'll have to let go and concentrate on our plan. Since this didn't go the way we wanted it, we'll have to call the Chinese. We can assure them that we'll be able to control the humans. After all, the gadget worked spectacularly well."

"I'm sorry." Telanuel fished a paper tissue from a box in the glove compartment and blew his nose. "I don't know what's wrong with me. Maybe it's all that magic tingling inside." But when he concentrated on the stolen magic, it was gone. Secretly he was quite relieved, so he didn't mention it.

"Never apologize! Dragons don't need to apologize, even if things don't go as planned." Mordekay took the next exit and headed for the mountains. "We'll simply adapt our plan. Call the Chinese ambassador. It's time to act."

Telanuel's flight took me by surprise. I hadn't expected to win so easily. Especially when he started crying, I wondered if the unblocking of his consciousness had something to do with this. I looked at the humans still kneeling and staring at the platform where the mayor, the hospital's administration, and the security guards all knelt. Everybody was staring at the space where just a moment ago Telanuel had ordered them around.

Only the governor was still running. His rotund form made it difficult, so no wonder that Telanuel had left him behind. The man was huffing, but Harm and Colin were already catching up to him while Luke was hurrying though the hospital's main entrance door. Maybe he had an inkling where Mordekay and the gadget would be.

Nicole stopped beside me and put her hands on her hips. "Well, I guess we'll have to unfreeze them."

"We might be able to use Luke's gadget," Meiming said. "He's a genius."

Soon, Harm and Colin returned with the governor. With blank eyes he stood there waiting for orders like a living doll. He creeped me out. The whole, unbelievably silent crowd creeped me out. Even the children were no longer running around playing. They also knelt and faced the podium.

A few minutes later, Luke returned empty-handed. "Mordekay managed to take it along. He left the laptop with the control program behind, but I'm sure he's got a copy. Without it, he can't activate the gadget. I'm sure he'll use it again. I saw them hightail it in a black limousine, probably the governor's."

I sighed. "In that case I'll have to unfreeze everybody individually. That'll take some time."

"I'll help." Meiming's blush looked cute. I understood why Luke had fallen for her. She seemed so very vulnerable.

I nodded to her. "I think it's best if we order everyone to forget this chaos."

Her face lit up. "I could make them remember the memory as it should have been."

I thought that a good idea. "Let's tell them to go to sleep until the planned end of the ceremony. That should give us enough time to treat them all."

We got to work. I started with the governor, and Meiming focused on the children. One by one, the humans fell into a nearly natural sleep, dreaming a ceremony that had never run its course. To make our lie believable, Harm and Colin dug a few cuts with the spade to truly break the ground.

Meiming came back. "I think I've got all you assigned to me. Only Isabella, Chelsea, and Patricia are missing. It's as if they walked away."

I wondered why my self-chosen enemy hadn't been affected by the gadget like everyone else. Could it be because I'd used my Commanding Voice on her back when she'd tried to bully me once too often and still hadn't withdrawn my order?

"I've got three more humans to do. Could you find the girls for me?" I asked Meiming. "I'll probably need to treat them separately." Most of all, I had to undo my last order. Surely it wasn't very healthy for a human to be under a dragon's control for so long, even if the dragon in question—me—hadn't known about the lasting command. Meiming only nodded and walked away in search of Isabella and her friends.

I was just telling the last person in my part of the crowd, a young mother with a sleeping baby in her arms, to go to sleep, when my mobile rang.

Longbow's ringtone! My heart seemed to stop, then raced. Something bad must have happened. He wouldn't call without reason. With shaking hands, I accepted the call.

"We're under attack." Longbow's voice sounded strained. "The Chinese came upon us undetected, so we couldn't gather all our forces. Although the Head of Council is doing her best to keep them from the castle, it's not looking too good. We need your help, Lydia."

"We'll be there as fast as we can." I waved to the others to come and asked Longbow, "Did you call Angie?"

"Yes, she's bringing Blackfeather. He's a great asset." Longbow spoke to someone behind him in a lowered voice before turning back to me. "My tribe is using nets to capture the Chinese. We think it better not to kill. They're not showing the same constraint."

"Try to keep as many people safe as you can." My hand cramped so hard it bent my mobile. "We're on our way."

"What kind of creature are you?" Isabella's voice made me whirl around. There she stood, slightly disheveled but healthy, with Patricia and Chelsea at her side. "Are *you* responsible for this?" She indicated the people sleeping while standing. "I always knew you're a real freak."

"And you were right." I didn't have the time to fight with her. Heck, I didn't have time for anything much. We had more important things to do.

I shifted, and Isabella's jaw dropped, followed by Patricia's and Chelsea's. None of the girls found their voice.

"I told you, you were right," I said. "Now, move aside, I need Colin and Nicole to climb up."

Harm shifted too and said, "Nicole hasn't gotten enough control over her powers yet. It's better that she stays here."

"Nice try." Nicole laughed and climbed onto Harm's back. "But I'm not sitting here in safety while you and my best friends are in danger."

Meiming was already waiting in dragon form with Luke on her back. We were ready to go. There was just one more thing. I turned to Isabella and her friends and removed the compulsion I'd put on them. Deciding I wouldn't force another spell on them, I tried to give them some good advice without sounding preachy. "You do know that no one will believe you if you tell them you saw dragons flying over the city, right?" Hopefully it would work.

With my thoughts already with my dragons, I took off. Harm and Meiming followed without hesitation. I flapped my wings to get high enough to vanish in the low-hanging clouds. When I glanced down a final time, Isabella was staring up at me. The expression of utter surprise was gone from her face, replaced by awe. When she realized I was looking, she lifted her hand and very slowly waved. I wondered if that meant her attitude toward me had changed. But the trouble my dragons were in pushed that thought aside, and I concentrated on flying faster than I'd ever flown before. I had to go home!

As soon as they reached the cloud cover, Meiming knew they were missing something. She increased her speed until she flew beside Lydia. "Luke needs his gear," she shouted over the wind. "I'll take him home. We'll follow as soon as possible."

Lydia nodded, her gaze on the horizon. Meiming could tell her heart was pulling her along. She felt the same pull. It was crucial to stop the fighting, but at the same time she needed to ensure that the man she loved wouldn't get killed. She swerved and raced back down toward the city.

To avoid detection, she used a spell that came naturally to her, one she'd used often in her life. Now everyone who chanced to look in their direction would gaze past them, ignoring what they might have seen. A spell like that cost less energy than a full invisibility spell. Meiming was pretty sure she'd need all of her energy soon.

They landed beside overflowing dumpsters in the dead-end alley behind Luke's apartment complex. Three rats ran away squealing, and Meiming pulled a face at the stench of used diapers, rotting food, and mixed chemicals. As soon as Luke had climbed off her back, she shifted. Hand in hand but silently, they ran the three flights up to Luke's home.

"Is that you, Theodore?" Illuminated by the flickering light of the TV screen, Luke's grandma stood in the frame of the living room's door and squinted into the small, semi-dark hall. The music and babbling from the TV made it hard to understand her.

"No, it's me, Luke." He spoke louder than usual, turned on the light, and pushed Meiming forward. "This is my girlfriend, Meiming."

His grandma cocked her head, then smiled. "You look nice, dear. Have we met before? It seems I've become quite forgetful."

Meiming bowed to her and answered politely like her mother had taught her. The knowledge and wisdom of the elderly was something she valued highly.

"She'll forget you as soon as her back is turned to you." A deep sadness filled Luke's voice. "Dementia, you know?"

His grandmother turned and walked into the living room. "I'm watching a rerun of Jeopardy, dear. Do you want to join me?"

"I'm sorry but we've got to leave soon," Luke said.

"I wasn't talking to you." She sat in her comfy chair and turned down the volume of the TV.

"I'm sorry but I have to help your grandson to put on his protective gear," Meiming said without thinking.

"Will you be fighting dragons, Luke?" The old lady bent sideways over her chair's armrest and gazed back at her grandchild with surprising clarity. Meiming could feel Luke's confusion. He nodded, and his grandmother continued. "In that case it's probably time to give you your heirloom. Fetch the box from the cupboard, Meiming." She pointed to a sideboard in the living room that was covered with photos of a man who looked just like Luke, only older. It must be her son, Luke's father. Meiming hurried over, opened the cabinet's doors and found a single, longish box. It was heavy but she managed to carry it to the old lady where she set it down beside her seat.

"This is all yours now, darling." The old lady touched the box with the tip of her oft-mended slipper.

Hesitantly, Luke opened the box. Meiming could see his eyes widen at the content. With reverence, he took a sword out and held it up. It glinted in the light, looking deadly and beautiful at the same time. Meiming admired the rubies set into the hilt, but the sleek silver of the blade itself sent shivers down her spine.

"Father's Dragonkiller." Luke spoke so low, Meiming barely heard him. "I thought it was lost when Dad…" His voice trailed off.

After a few silent seconds, he returned his attention to the box with a jerk. He pulled out a short lance and a dagger with a glass vial set into its hilt. The vial was filled with a liquid that made Meiming shiver. He got up and kissed his grandmother's cheek. "Thank you, Gran."

"Promise you'll return alive." Tears ran down her cheeks. "I can bear losing you too."

"I swear."

Meiming wasn't surprised to see tears in Luke's eyes too, even though she thought the promise was rather foolish. No one knew what would happen when they fought the Chinese.

Pain shot through her heart. She didn't really want to fight them. After all, she was responsible for their loss. But she couldn't stand by and let her friends bear the consequences. "We'd better hurry," she said to Luke, who was still hugging his grandmother. He nodded and let go. They'd barely left the living room when the sound of the TV rose to its previous level again.

Fourteenth Chapter

*W*ordlessly, Meiming helped Luke into his chainmail. When she reached for metal shinpads, Luke shook his head. "Those are only for show or if one has to fight a single dragon. In a war like the one we're facing, their weight would slow me down too much." He grabbed a helmet and headed for the door.

Meiming followed him into the tiny hall, when Luke's grandmother called. "Meiming?"

She walked into the living room and bent down.

The old lady's eyes were hard as pebbles. "Swear that you'll bring him back alive."

"I'll do my best," Meiming said.

"If you, as a dragon, won't promise, you must be in deep trouble." The grandmother blinked several times, and Meiming's heart contracted. How could the old lady know she was a dragon? Luke's grandma winked at her. "I'm a dragon slayer's wife, mother, and grandmother. Don't you think I've learned to spot them? But don't worry. I won't tell anyone, and I'm sure

Luke already knows. I've always said that most dragons aren't as bad as my husband and Theodore made them out to be."

"Thank you," Meiming whispered. She didn't know what else to say.

"I don't want to know about the trouble you're in." Luke's grandmother took her hands. Her eyes were haunted. "At least promise me you'll tell me if something happens to Luke. The knowledge might kill me, but not knowing would be worse."

Meiming understood. She nodded, pressed the palms of her hands together in front of her chest and bowed. "I swear I will personally come by to tell you," she promised.

A few minutes later, they were airborne again.

Meiming struggled with the added weight. She'd never carried someone so heavy. All that iron was threatening to drag her back down to earth, and maintaining the don't-see-me spell took its toll too. She panted and flapped the vestigial wings on her feet harder to create additional lift.

"You can do this, my darling." Her mother's voice in her ear startled her. Meiming looked around but she was alone in the sky. Again her mother spoke, even though she wasn't visible. "Remember the center of gravity."

Oh yes, how often had they trained that. Meiming closed her eyes and focused. She felt for the white whirling of her center and breathed deeply. In, one – two – three, out, one – two – three. After but a few gasps, new strength filled her. She opened her eyes and increased her speed. Instinctively Luke bent forward until he was lying on her back. With the decrease of air resistance, they flew even faster. Soon, Meiming could see the mountains that housed the biggest colony of European dragons in North America. So far, the fight with the Chinese wasn't visible, but she feared the worst. As fast as she could, she headed for Lydia's castle. Their friends needed them.

Harm dropped Nicole close to the gigantic doors of the castle, where she hid behind a huge flower carved into the wall. The air behind it smelled stale and dusty. When she put her hand against the stone, she realized with a shock that the tiny flames were back, dancing over her arms. Had her magic grown back this fast? That wasn't possible, or was it? The flames ended a little above her left wrist where the strange bracelet should be that connected her to Meiming. She still wasn't sure what it was good for, but as long as it kept the flames at bay even a little, she didn't worry.

The distant roaring of dragons slowly drawing nearer ripped her from her thoughts. She concentrated on what was happening on the landing platform again. Surely she'd have to use her magic soon anyway, and that would keep the flames at bay. But a trace of worry remained, and she couldn't shake it.

Colin slipped behind a similar flower on the other side of the gate while Lydia walked toward the front of the landing platform. The Head of Council stood there in her dragon form, bent forward, obviously straining to listen.

Harm herded a group of much smaller dragons toward the gate, but the dragonets resisted. He ordered the smaller dragons to go into the castle.

"But we want to help Lydia," the smallest squealed.

"You help her best if you stay inside the castle. Dragonets aren't strong enough to fight fully grown dragons." He looked stern, but Nicole noticed that his face mellowed when he realized how upset the youngsters truly were. "Very well, I know something you can do to really help Lydia."

Seven expectant faces looked up at him.

"Lock every door of the castle, even the ones the Nuciu use, so no one can come inside." He smiled and the dragonets visibly relaxed.

It took Nicole a moment to remember that the Native Americans protecting the dragons called themselves Nuciu. She was impressed at how well Harm handled the children.

He continued. "You're our future. Your parents and Lydia need you to be safe. So show her how grown up you already are and lock up the castle until either Lydia or I tell you to open up again."

The dragonets nodded like one and hurried to close the gate. Of course they needed Harm's help. When only a small opening remained, they slipped through. A few heartbeats later, the gate thudded closed.

"The Nuciu will make sure they remain safe even if we can't stop the Chinese." Harm pressed his lips together. Nicole could tell how worried he was. He looked at her with his wonderful, warm blue eyes filled with concern. "Stay hidden. The fight is drawing nearer, and a single human will get trampled underfoot. If you can, use your magic to help Lydia."

"Will do." She smiled up at him, trying to ease his worry. "And you'll do your best to stay alive." It wasn't a question, but a statement.

Harm nodded and took off again. Nicole watched him go, then turned her attention to Lydia, who seemed to be discussing the war with the Head of Council. Despite the distance, she could hear words like *tactic, approaching,* and *fierce.* Lydia was mostly listening.

Then the sounds of fighting grew louder and louder.

A yellow dragon came flying with a turquoise Chinese dragon dangling from its claws.

"Open the dungeon," the yellow dragon called, and the Head of Council flicked her wing. A hole opened right in front of her. The yellow dragon swooped in and dropped the Chinese dragon low over it. But instead of falling right in, the captive twisted mid-air and headed toward Lydia and the Head of Council.

"Death to the usurper!" he cried. His voice wasn't much deeper than that of the dragonets Harm had secured. He hurled something at Lydia.

Instinctively, Nicole shoved a wave of magic outward. The round object was a balloon filled with a liquid. It bounced off of her shield and broke on impact with the ground. The contents splattered everywhere. A few drops hit the Chinese dragon's tail, and he screamed with pain. He writhed in pain, and small tendrils of smoke rose from his tail where the drops had hit him.

"Dragon Bane bombs!" Lydia gasped and waved to the yellow dragon. "Tell everyone … Duh, don't bother. I'll do it myself." She shook her head, closed her eyes, and focused. "Beware! The Chinese have Dragon Bane bombs." Her voice sounded directly in Nicole's head. How cool was that? She grinned. Her friend surprised her over and over again.

Lydia walked to the Chinese dragon. The yellow dragon had grabbed him again and was pressing him to the ground. She bent down to him, but the Chinese dragon obviously wasn't up to talking. His screams grew louder by the second. Nicole's heart went out to him. He was barely more than a child, for crying out loud.

She gazed around but there wasn't much to do right now, so she hurried from her hiding place to where Lydia and the injured dragon were. She put her hands on the writhing form. Luckily the yellow dragon still held him pinned to the ground so the captive couldn't hurt her accidentally. Closing her eyes, she focused on the dragon's magic. The coolness of a bath in a summer lake welcomed her, but the ripples of pain could already be felt.

"You're a water dragon," Nicole urged the youngster. His self was still vague and hovering over the lake like a fluffy cloud. "Use that. Wash away the pain."

"I can't." He flew circles and wailed.

"I'll help you, but the longer you wait, the harder it gets." Nicole decided that another magical wave would be the best. She shoved the dragon's watery-feeling magic with her own toward the circling cloudy dragon. All of a sudden, the young dragon blinked into view, as if someone had finally finished the painting. He grabbed the soothing wetness Nicole had directed at him and hurled it somewhere she had no access to.

"More," he called, and Nicole complied.

After several repetitions of the procedure, the young dragon sank to the ground and closed his eyes. His watery-feeling magic ran low, but at least he wasn't wailing any longer. Had it worked?

She opened her eyes and looked around. The yellow dragon had left, and the young Chinese was lying limp on the ground. The area around him swam with water, and Colin was busy wiping away the rest of the Dragon Bane with a broom he'd fashioned from a couple of young trees.

"What did you save him for?" The Head of Council, who'd dragged Lydia a few steps back, frowned. "He's our enemy."

"If it were your dragonet, wouldn't you want someone to help him too?" Nicole got to her feet and looked around. The noise of the fighting dragons had increased again, so the grumbling of her stomach was barely audible.

"You've done well. We're no monsters," Lydia said. "But the Chinese see us that way. We need a plan to stop the fighting, so we can explain about Mordekay and Telanuel."

The young Chinese dragon moaned.

"Maybe we can use him as a messenger." Nicole pulled an energy bar from one of her pockets, ripped it open and ate. Simultaneously she sucked energy from the ground since the sun was still hidden behind a wall of clouds.

A dark blue dragon with silver beard and fringe hair shot out from the trees, chased by a pair of bronze dragons. When he noticed the young dragon lying motionless on the ground in front of Nicole, he howled.

"My son!" He twisted mid-air and raced toward her with open jaws, ready to swallow her.

Dropping her energy bar, she raised her hands, and with them a solid wall of compacted air. Rather satisfied, she noticed that the flames on her arms were as good as gone. *The training with Herbert has been extremely useful,* she thought as the blue dragon slammed into her shield. He landed, shaking his head, but turned toward her again in a heartbeat. The two bronze dragons that had been chasing him had finally corrected their direction and were now upon him. Before he could jump Nicole, they launched themselves at him and nailed him to the ground.

"That's the Chinese ambassador," the Head of Council said. "Search him. He might have another one of those Dragon Bane bombs."

Lydia harrumphed, and the Head of Council took a step back. "I'm sorry, Your Majesty. It happened by habit."

"I understand, but I'm acting queen now. At least temporarily." Lydia stepped forward until she was standing right beside the group of dragons. All of a sudden Nicole felt tiny and insignificant, but that feeling passed when Lydia spoke.

"Your son tried to kill me with a Dragon Bane bomb. He was thwarted and got hit by the poison. It would have been his end if my friend Nicole hadn't helped him." She pointed to the young dragon. "I don't know if he'll survive, but his chances are much better because of her help."

The Chinese ambassador slumped, and Lydia waved for the bronze dragons to take a step back. "Now, if you don't mind, we need to talk." She turned into a human and held out her hand.

Nicole thought the gesture crazy, and the Head of Council obviously too because she gasped. But instead of attacking, the Chinese ambassador turned into a human too and took the offered hand.

"May I see to my son first?" His face showed two deep lines of concern on his otherwise smooth features. "He's my only child. I didn't even know he'd come."

"Certainly." Lydia took a step back.

The Chinese ambassador pulled two small balloons from his pockets that were filled with a liquid, most likely Dragon Bane. Immediately all the surrounding dragons stepped backward; only Colin and Nicole stepped forward to stand in front of Lydia. The Chinese handed the wobbly balloons to Colin, who dumped them into the open pit, looking at Lydia with a cheeky grin. "You don't need the dungeon anymore anyway, right?"

Lydia ginned back and shook her head. It was only good that there weren't any dragons in the dungeon right now.

The Chinese ambassador took a step toward his son, but then stopped and turned back to Lydia. "I am sorry we took

141

these weapons. Mordekay assured us they'd only paralyze you. We're not out to kill the last queen there still is."

"There are queens in Africa and South America too," Lydia reminded him. "Only Australia doesn't have any."

"We know, but to evade extinction, we need someone related to us. I'll explain later." He turned back to his son, crouched, and examined his wounds. Shaking his head, he mumbled, "Only a few drops so tiny…"

Nicole stared at the ambassador. He seemed friendly enough and his worry over his son seemed genuine, but then, he was a diplomat. He'd probably learned to control his feelings. Nicole decided to be on the watch. She sucked up some more energy from the ground to be ready should he try anything foolish while Lydia kept talking to him.

"Dragon Bane is probably the most dangerous poison for dragons in the whole world. And I'm sure Mordekay deliberately told you a lie. As far as we know he's the only dragon who's ever been able to actually lie." Lydia walked up to him and put a hand on his shoulder. "He also lied to you when he told you that I sent the messenger with the poison."

"I know that now." The Chinese ambassador looked up, fighting tears and stroking his son's lightly twitching tail.

"Then let us stop this war." Again, Lydia held out a hand. "It costs lives neither side can afford to lose."

"I'm sorry for this." In a heartbeat, the ambassador turned into his dragon form, grabbed Lydia, and took off.

FIFTEENTH CHAPTER

*J*ust a yard off the ground, he slammed into another one of Nicole's shields, but this time, the shield folded around him, passing over Lydia, and pinned him down beside his son. Lydia bounced off his chest and slipped onto the ground beside him. Nicole was rather proud that she'd anticipated his move.

The ambassador's son struggled to raise his head. His turquoise scales stood off of his face, and he stared at his father with surprise. "What did you do that for? They saved my life."

The ambassador didn't answer.

Lydia got up and dusted her jeans off. "You need a queen, and he probably thought that I could be persuaded or forced into the job if he took me."

"But why?" The youngster looked confused, something Nicole picked up on although she found it hard to read dragon expressions.

"It's a question of power control. Imagine dragons trying democracy." Lydia laughed. "We'd never get anything done."

The Head of Council growled. "That's not funny. I suggest throwing the kidnapper into the dungeon. There should be enough Dragon Bane down there to take care of the problem."

Lydia lost her mirth instantly. "My tribe will not murder a desperate person, be it man or dragon." She opened her mouth to continue, but Nicole stopped her.

"Look there. Meiming!" She pointed to the sky above where a white Chinese dragon with a seemingly gray human rider was speeding toward them, followed by a teal dragon who was spitting fire. It was gaining on Meiming.

Lydia's eyes went wide. "Stop that," she called to the teal dragon and it obeyed. Still, it kept hovering over Meiming. The Chinese dragon sank to the ground close to the captured ambassador and his son. The father's eyes opened wide and his jaw dropped. He seemed to be gagging on words that never came.

Luke hopped off of Meiming, pulled a wicked-looking sword, turned and ran toward the forest's edge. Only now did Nicole notice that the sounds of the fight had come closer the whole time. She could already make out individual dragons between the trees that were biting, buffeting, and scratching each other. Flames turned trees into torches, and ice or water drenched the ground. It was chaos complete.

She had to stop the destruction from coming closer. Since she couldn't separate the species, she concentrated on erecting a barrier between the fight and the castle. Better than nothing.

A wobbly balloon sped toward the group of dragons. Nicole felt the magic that was used to propel it forward, and tried to get her barrier up before it passed her defense, but she was too late. The barrier snapped into place as the balloon descended on Meiming.

A turquoise flash rose in front of Meiming.

The Dragon Bane bomb slammed into the young dragon's chest. The ambassador's son got drenched by the poison, but not a single drop of the dangerous liquid reached one of the other dragons. The youngster must have used magic to draw all the poison onto himself. His scream rang in Nicole's ears.

Water began to pour out of him, flooding the whole area but miraculously evading Meiming. Was the dying dragon responsible for this? Colin grabbed her and dragged her toward Lydia and the Head of Council.

The young dragon's scream went on and on and the stench of charcoal and burnt meat filled the air, making it hard for Nicole to concentrate. She pushed the scream, the stench, and the maintaining of the barrier aside, and focused on the dying dragon. Shoving as much magic into him as she could, she examined his injuries. The poison had eaten away most of his skin and was already spreading in his blood stream. All she could do was ease his pain.

She encapsulated the pain center of his brain, and his screaming stopped. He sank to the ground beside his father, who was writhing and twisting, trying to break free from Nicole's spell.

She double-checked that it was still strong enough. After all, the ambassador would die too should he touch his son.

The ambassador's son glanced to Nicole, breathing hard. "Thank you," he mouthed. His flesh burned and charcoal clouds rose to the sky.

By now, the stench was so strong, Nicole's stomach cramped. It was clear that the young dragon's end was close. She bit her lip to stop from crying. *What an evil way to die,* she thought. *He could have become a friend.* She poured more magic into him, trying to make his end as painless as she could. He relaxed. His last smile was directed at his father. "Look at her," he whispered, nodding toward Meiming. "She looks just like my wife. Talk to them, Dad. For Jun Ling and me."

"Wong!" The ambassador's voice broke and tears ran over his face.

The young dragon murmured something in Chinese, then sank back, staring sightlessly into the sky. His heart had stopped beating, but vile, black smoke was still rising from his chest.

Nicole wiped away her tears, which wasn't easy since new ones welled up all the time. However, there was still the issue of the fighting dragons. "How many more of these bombs do your people have?" she asked the ambassador, and her voice sounded harsh even in her own ears.

"We had ten to start with but one was lost in the forest somewhere." He answered without looking at her. "Please set me free. I won't flee, I promise. I just want to hold my son."

"That'd kill you too." She ignored his pleas and turned to the forest. *Six bombs left …* She would never, ever allow anything like the young dragon's death to happen again. Closing her eyes, she sucked up energy from the ground, from the sky, and from the forest. At the same time, she wracked her brain for an idea how to stop the killing. Harm was out there, fighting, and so were Luke and Longbow and a lot of the Nuciu. Grinding her teeth, she concentrated and opened her eyes. She would end the dragon war if it killed her.

When the balloon shot toward her, Meiming had stepped back involuntarily, but only when the young dragon began to scream did she realize the balloon had been filled with Dragon Bane. Without hesitation she followed Colin to Lydia, who was still in

146

her human form, but her gaze was glued to the dying youngster. The black smoke coiling from his chest stank of burnt meat and rotten vegetables, nauseating her.

"We must stop this," she whispered.

Lydia agreed, staring at the forest's edge. "I've already tried to recall the dragons of my tribe, but they won't listen."

"You called?" Meiming looked at her with surprise. "I didn't hear anything."

"I can talk to them in my mind." Lydia's face lit up. "Why don't we do it together? I tell *my*dragons to stop, and you tell yours. You should be able to do that. After all, you truly are the last Chinese princess."

"I don't know how." Meiming shifted into her human form and took Lydia's hand. "But if you show me, I'll do my best."

"Protect us," Lydia said to the Head of Council. "We don't have much time if we want both tribes to survive."

"I'll do my best," the Head of Council said.

The two girls huddled behind a statue, closed their eyes, and entered the realm of magic once more. The stench of the dead dragon vanished, and the white nothingness welcomed them. It seemed freshly washed.

Meiming breathed deeply. "This looks so much brighter than before. What happened?"

"Your friend helped me back," a familiar, warm alto voice said behind her.

Meiming's heart raced and she hot around. "Mama!" She hurled herself into her mother's arms. "How can this be?"

"We don't have much time," Lydia reminded her. "We need to reconnect you with the magic Telanuel stole. We've got to stop a war, remember?"

"I'll explain later," Son Ling said. "The first step will be to free your grandmother and great-grandmother."

"They're here too?" Meiming's heart felt ready to burst with happiness when her mother nodded. Even the memory of the young dragon's death couldn't cloud that happiness for long.

Together they shifted, and flew into the snowy realm side by side. For once the weather was sunny. Wide fields of snow covered the flanks of the mountains. Their peaks reached for the sky, and Meiming's breath condensed in the icy air. To her surprise, her mother's didn't emit such clouds.

"I'm only a remnant, barely more than a memory of me," Son Ling said when Meiming asked. She landed on a small plateau with a snow-filled dip that was surrounded by boulders. "Here we are."

Meiming looked around, but no one was in sight and the snow wasn't broken. No one had walked here for a while. But when she meant to point that out to her mother, she noticed that the other dragon didn't leave footprints either. She looked around some more. Lydia was gone, but somehow footprints appeared close to two boulders leaning against each other. Even if she couldn't see her, it had to be Lydia.

Meiming walked over. "What do I have to do?"

Warm fingers touched her hand, and Lydia said, "Here, can you feel the chains?"

Meiming groped something that seemed to be a chain made of a very smooth stone. She nodded.

"I tried to break it, but it's attuned to you only." Lydia's voice and her footprints were right beside her. "You need to break them."

Resistance built up in Meiming's mind like a wall of bricks. "It'd be a pity to destroy such craftsmanship."

Lydia sighed. "If you break a single chain link, the rest can be preserved, but your ancestors would be free. Come on. Overcome the compulsion Telanuel put on you."

Meiming's finger tightened around one chain link. Everything inside of her screamed to let go and run. Something bad would happen if she broke the link. Fighting the adamant voice in her own head, she told herself, "I trust Lydia," over and over again. But only when the glowing bracelet on her wrist lit up did she find the strength she needed. With a short, strong twist of her hands, she broke the link. It ripped open as easily as if she'd simply snapped a thread.

Loud clinking made her look up with surprise. Two snow-white Chinese dragons and Lydia appeared, and only the young queen's legs broke the snow's surface. Meiming's heart beat faster and faster. The two new dragons seemed awfully familiar even though she'd never met them. She'd felt their love her whole life. Wordlessly, she hugged them, first the one with the orange hairs, then the one with the turquoise.

After a few moments of stunned silence, everyone started to talk at once.

"Meiming, darling."

"Grandma, great-grandma!"

"Where did you...?"

"How could you...?"

"We've got so much..." and more. The words echoed through the mountain air.

"Stop it," Lydia said. "We'll still need to reconnect this realm with the realm of Queen's Magic if Meiming and I are to stop the war. I know there's a very thin connection. Your ancestors told me so."

"A war?" Again all the dragons talked at once, but Meiming cut them short.

"Lydia is right. Let's find this connection."

Shifting back to her dragon form, Meiming flew to and fro, sniffing and feeling for a dribble of magic. The other dragons followed her example.

In the end, it was Lydia who discovered it. "Over here," she called.

When Meiming and her ancestors reached the place, they found themselves in front of a small mountain lake. Its motionless silvery surface reflected the blue sky and surrounding mountain tops like a mirror. Only at the spot where Lydia was standing did tiny ripples move the water.

"This is where the magic comes in," Lydia said. "I can feel the gap, but I'm too big to squeeze through. You'll have to go first and widen the way for me."

Meiming's stomach knotted. She'd never been very happy under water. She was an ice dragon, after all. But then she told herself that ice was just a different form of water, breathed in deeply, and plunged into the lake.

It was much deeper than it had appeared from outside, and the banks dropped nearly vertically. Meiming dove deeper and deeper, following a current that got stronger the deeper she went. Finally, when the water had already grown quite dark, she discovered a vertical slit in the rocky bank where water and magic squirted out. It was just big enough for her to squeeze through. Forcing herself into the narrow cave, the rocks around her moved aside and the cavity widened. She pushed on.

After a while, her lungs screamed for air. If she didn't find some soon, she'd suffocate. *I can't do this,* she thought. *I don't have enough air anymore!*

"Stay calm." The voice behind her was that of her great-grandmother. "Remember that this is not really water but your magic and that of your ancestors. Just breathe normally and trust us, and you will be able to continue.

Fighting instinct was the hardest thing Meiming had ever done. No one could breathe under water—except mermaids, should they be more than a legend. Still, she trusted her great-grandma without question. Very, very carefully, she let out some stale air and breathed in. Fresh air flowed into her lungs, and she gasped with relief. Then she continued to squeeze herself through the narrow gap. It kept widening behind her.

Inching herself forward, she noticed a light up ahead. Even though the tunnel she was crawling though grew smaller with every foot, it became easier to move forward. She didn't need to shift into her much smaller human form. She felt as if someone or something was pulling her toward the light.

Diving into the circle of light, she rolled into a meadow with a sucking plop. When she looked up, countless dragon faces stared back at her.

A white Chinese dragon with a fringe of golden hair was the first to speak. "You look like my daughter."

A turquoise dragon squeezed past the others and helped her to her feet. It was the ambassador's son.

"Meiming!" He hugged her. "My wife will be delighted to finally meet you." He turned toward the gathered dragons and pushed Meiming gently forward. "Welcome the lost princess."

Meiming protested. After all, it had been her great-grandmother who had abandoned the Chinese dragons, but in the clamor of welcoming voices her words were lost. It was even a struggle to remain close to the place where she'd entered this realm. She turned to look at the place, and stared, unbelieving, at a dark hole that hung in the air over a warm summer meadow. The air around it rippled and twisted, as if something big was pushing against it from the inside.

With another plop, her great-grandmother appeared, hugged and kissed immediately by her parents. She was followed by Meiming's mother and grandmother. The hole grew bigger with every ejection. With a final heave, it spat out Lydia's huge dragon form. A white and a golden dragon hurried to her side and hugged her. She held them close.

All of a sudden, Meiming felt very lonely. *If only Luke were here,* she thought. *He'd love this place.* She walked to the hole that still hung in the air. Its edges shivered and rippled as if it were ready to collapse. An urge inside made her poke the rim, and the air around it shivered. The hole caved in.

Completely soundlessly, the realm shifted and expanded. Part of the hills with their flower meadows and babbling brooks were pushed aside and the craggy mountains of Meiming's magical realm appeared. Suddenly everybody was standing beside the small mountain lake Meiming had come through.

Something in her heart exploded. It felt so right to be here. Joyfully she turned to Lydia. "We did it." She grinned, only wishing she could share this happiness with Luke. "I'm finally fully home."

"True, but the war's not over yet," Lydia said. "We need to return to reality and order all the dragons to stop fighting."

SIXTEENTH CHAPTER

When Meiming and Lydia withdrew into themselves, Nicole's skin prickled as the two dragons' magic vanished. A quick scan of her arms showed that her own magic hadn't diminished significantly. Tiny flames licked at her skin. Still, it was exhausting to bundle the power and use it. Nicole did her best to keep the barrier up against the chaos of war.

Colin wordlessly dragged the dead dragon's remains to a small brook of water running under her barrier. He pushed the body in and the stinking, black smoke grew thinner and thinner the more Dragon Bane was washed away. Nicole was very grateful for that. He also fetched a bucket from somewhere and washed the Dragon Bane that had splashed on the ground down into the dungeons. Finally, Nicole could take the restraints off the ambassador. The blue dragon immediately crouched beside his son's body next to the brook and began to sing a haunting, sad song.

Nicole pushed more of her magic into her barrier, since the fight was comnig ever closer. Although there were far more dragons from Lydia's tribe on the battlefield, the Chinese were obviously winning. Most European dragons bled from many wounds. Some were so weak that others had to carry them.

Nicole adjusted her magic to let the wounded and their rescuers through her shield, but only very few of the rescuers remained in safety. Most put down the badly wounded at the rim of the platform in front of the castle and returned to the fight. Nicole wanted to call them back, but she needed all her strength to keep up the barrier.

A loud crash drew her attention to a pair of dragons fighting to her left, not far from the brook. Her heart stuttered as she recognized Harm, who'd just slammed a Chinese dragon against a tree. The Chinese dragon retaliated by levitating water from the brook in a big bubble and aiming it at Harm's head. Nicole wanted to call out, but Harm had already seen the danger. A stream of flame evaporated most of the water. The rest fell harmlessly to the ground.

Nicole forced herself to look away. Right now it was her duty to protect Lydia's and Meiming's bodies. She'd help Harm as soon as they were back. She glanced at the two girls lying behind one of the statues carved into the front of the palace. They still weren't moving. *Oh, come on,* she thought. *Hurry up already. This is exhausting.* She bit into the energy bar again and sucked more strength from the ground.

She needed so much power, the soil below her feet was slowly getting drained. Of course there was strength flowing back from the sides, Nicole could feel it, but it was too slow. Maintaining her shield, she looked up. Where was the sun? The steady drizzle and the gray cloud cover didn't give her much hope, so she walked a little bit along the platform's rim. It was hard to keep up the shield, but fresh energy poured into her. Relieved, she glanced at Harm. He was already bleeding from a couple of minor wounds, but he'd managed to subdue the Chinese dragon. He pressed him down with all his strength. Just when he reached for a boulder to knock him unconscious, a small object wobbled through the air toward him.

Immediately, Nicole began to push her barrier outward to stop the Dragon Bane bomb, but a magical object this big was hard to move. Also, the bracelet connecting her with Meiming sucked off a major amount of magic right at that moment. Nicole swore silently.

"Harm!" Nicole's scream made him turn and notice the projectile. Instinctively he threw himself sideways and pushed the captured dragon to the other side. The Chinese skidded over the ground and landed in the brook, just as the Dragon Bane bomb splattered on the ground. It had happened so fast, Nicole hadn't managed to push her shield out far enough.

Harm howled as splashes of the poison seared his skin.

With a scream of frustration and sorrow, Nicole dropped her shield and ran toward Harm. He was thrashing around in pain. As she neared him, she realized that only a few drops of Dragon Bane had splashed against his chest. That should count for something, shouldn't it? They'd saved the ambassador's son with more splashes than that the first time. Her heart hammered in her chest as she tried to find a way to put her hand on Harm, but her beloved thrashed around so strongly that she couldn't get near.

The Chinese dragon was just crawling out of the brook with murder in his eyes, hovering a gigantic bubble of water over his head.

"Oh no, you don't," Nicole whispered. She lashed out with her magic. The bubble burst, dousing the Chinese, Harm and her. Most of the Dragon Bane was washed away. As the attacker rose again to pounce on Harm, a group of Chinese dragons hurried toward the castle. Obviously they'd noticed that her shield was gone. Anger coursed through her. Her breathing got ragged. She narrowed her burning eyes. First Harm, now the rest of her friends? She wouldn't allow that. She gathered all the strength she could get from the ground and pushed her magic outward. Like a fist, it slammed down on the group approaching the castle and on the Chinese dragon who was nosediving toward Harm with extended claws.

She felt them squirm and push against her spell with their own magic. Boy, were they strong. She struggled to hold them down, sucking even more energy from the ground. Sparing some of that energy, she sent a tendril of her magic out to examine the Chinese's magic. Something felt strange yet familiar. Her tendril poked the Chinese's magic, and her eyes widened. *They pool their magic. That's why they're winning against a superior force.* With a few more probes, she'd found the dragon who was channeling and wielding the magic. With a satisfied sigh, she slammed an invisible weight onto his head. He passed out immediately. As she had guessed, none of the other dragons was prepared to take over. She grabbed the magic and added it to her own as if she'd never done anything else. She even ignored the fact that the flames on her arms were now nearly a foot in height. It was better dying for what she believed to be right than to live without Harm and her friends. The worry about Harm threatened to overwhelm her at this thought, but she managed to push it aside for the moment. She needed some space to focus on saving him, and she was determined to get it.

"It's time to end this war," she said, more to herself than to anyone else. She was very angry with the pig-headed dragons. *If only they'd started talking in time to prevent this.* She lifted her hands, palms up, and creepers shot from the ground, binding friend and foe alike, regardless where in the big forest they were. They also sucked magic from all the dragons like leeches, adding it to her own pool. The flames on her arms grew and her skin began to hurt. She'd have to give it back soon, or she'd burn to death. But right now, she needed everyone to remain in place. Since that meant no attempt to escape with magic, she had to hold onto it no matter how much it hurt.

Finally she was able to reach Harm. Even half-drowned and tied down, his body was still twitching madly. Tears ran over Nicole's cheeks. She needed to heal him, but that would mean letting go of the spell holding down the dragons. The flames on her arms flared up to three feet in height as her heart fought with her consciousness. Love and war or loneliness and peace?

A warm hand touched her arm for a short moment. The Chinese ambassador crouched beside her in his human form. "Keep them from fighting. I'll help your friend." He put both his hands on Harm's chest and closed his eyes. A strange golden glow illuminated his fingers.

Why isn't he tied down? Nicole looked around and noticed that the tendrils she'd called forth had only grown in the soil surrounding the platform, not on the rock itself. That was the reason why the ambassador hadn't been tied down too and why he'd retained his magic. To her surprise, his glow seemed to relax Harm. The young dragon's body stopped writhing, but his breathing was still ragged.

Sweat beaded on the ambassador's forehead, and he panted. "This is the worst poison I've ever encountered," he said. "It keeps burning deeper and deeper into the flesh even though there's less than a drop left in your friend's massive body."

Nicole shivered as she imagined a life without Harm. Compared to the pain of that thought, the nipping of the flames on her arms was insignificant. Harm *had* to survive. Letting him die just wouldn't do. Closing her eyes for a short moment, she reached out with her tendril of magic and found the ambassador's magic without a problem. Gathering the magic she'd stolen from all the dragons, she poured it into the ambassador's pool.

He gasped and stared at her wide-eyed with his mouth hanging open. Then he shook his head as if to clear it and returned to the task at hand.

Luke ran through the forest, looking for Telanuel and Mordekay. He knew that Meiming would want to keep her foster father safe even if he'd gone rogue. And Mordekay had to be taken down. Luke didn't mean to keep the black dragon alive. He'd caused too much trouble already. Of course, death wasn't the best punishment—Luke would have preferred something long and painful—but it would be too dangerous to let Mordekay live.

So he raced past the fighting dragons. The snake-like bodies of the Chinese wound around the plumper ones of their European-American cousins. Streams of fire and acid filled the air, and trees were burning or smoking all around them.

It took all of Luke's agility to evade the dragons' spit, but he didn't give up. He only stopped once to wind a piece of cloth around the lower part of his face to keep from choking, and then ran on. He zigzagged between the fighters, lashing out with his father's dragon slayer here and there to clear the way. Telanuel and Mordekay were nowhere in sight. Were they cowards who stayed behind and let others do their dirty work?

Whenever a dragon or two passed overhead, Luke stopped to see if it was one of the dragons he was looking for, but mostly he witnessed two or more of Lydia's dragons chasing a Chinese. By rights, Lydia's side should have been winning, but he had the distinct feeling that this wasn't the case.

Evading another cloud of heated acid, he raced uphill. Maybe he could see the fighters better when he was further up. Soon he reached a rocky slope that led higher and higher. After a few yards, it widened considerably and the trees grew lass numerous and finally vanished completely except for some crippled growths clinging to cracks in the rock. The higher he climbed, the steeper the ground fell off to his right. He had a good view of the forest below. Trees were burning everywhere. Lydia would have to contain the fires soon or human firefighters would show up. Panting hard from the exertion, Luke bent forward and scrutinized the dragons. There were a few green ones, but none of them was black.

He was just about to turn back when he noticed movement slightly higher up. There were clearly some dragons. With a start he realized that whoever hid there was right above the dragon clan's castle, which also meant right above Lydia and Meiming.

As quietly as he could, he crept uphill, using rocks and the few bushes as cover. Luckily the wind was coming down the mountains, so the dragons wouldn't smell him until he was very close.

On the plateau, a Native American equipped with bow and arrows was dancing between two dragons, one black, the other green, who tried to fry the young fighter. They always missed. Luke had never seen a fighter this fast.

Whenever the man found a little cover, he let one of his arrows fly. Telanuel's wings already showed a couple of rips, but Mordekay was unharmed.

"I've had about enough." Mordekay snorted. "These puny humans are everywhere. Tell him to stay still."

"I'm immune to the Commanding Voice," the Native American said. "I'm the queen's bodyguard, and you will not pass me for as long as I live."

Another arrow hissed through the air. Mordekay stepped aside, right into the path of a second arrow. Although it only had a stone head, it buried itself deeply into his shoulder. He screamed with the pain. "I'm going to kill all humans," he roared and hurled himself toward the Native American.

Luke was sure that the young man was perfectly capable of taking care of himself, so he focused on Telanuel. The green dragon had stepped back until he was standing very close to the rocky cliff. He was shaking his head from side to side. Although Luke still found it hard to read dragon expressions, something was definitely going on in the green dragon's mind. His features changed constantly.

As fast as he could, he crawled close. His gut told him that Telanuel was up to something, and that he had to get as close as possible to prevent whatever he was planning.

Just as he slipped behind a boulder not three feet away from the dragon, Telanuel opened his wings and shook them. "This is all wrong! Never should one dragon clan fight another!"

"Stop getting a fit and help me kill this human," Mordekay said.

"No." Telanuel shifted into his human form. He pulled two Dragon Bane bombs from a bag that hung over his shoulder and flung them toward Mordekay. "You're a devil in disguise. Die!"

The bombs hit the ground close to the Native American and Mordekay, splattering both with a generous dose. Nothing happened.

Mordekay's laugh drowned out every other sound atop the plateau. "You forgot that I've got an antidote. How else do you think I was able to handle the stuff?"

Telanuel's beard quivered and tears were running over his face. "Because of you I've committed crimes I never thought possible. Because of you, dragon is fighting dragon. Because of you, I lost Meiming. My life is worth nothing any more. Please, Meiming, forgive me." He stepped backward and spread his arms. Another inch and he'd fall.

Luke shot forward and slammed into the man, knocking him sideways to safety. Telanuel howled. He jumped to his feet at the same time as Luke, and tried to get past him to the cliff's edge. Luke held on as best he could. Being so much heavier, Telanuel dragged him along inch by inch.

The cliff came closer and closer.

Seventeenth Chapter

"*P*lease, Telanuel. Don't." Luke panted. "Meiming would be devastated."

"She's dead!" Howling, Telanuel jerked them even closer to the edge. Only a few more inches …

"No, she's not." Luke put his feet against a small rock sticking out from the ground, and threw himself backward. It was hard to talk while holding on to a desperately struggling man. "We saved her and tricked you."

"Liar!" Telanuel twisted in his grip and threw himself over the cliff. Pain shot through Luke's arms. He didn't let go, not even when he lost his footing. Together they shot out into the air and fell toward the castle's landing platform below them, but only Luke was screaming. Mordekay's satisfied laugh followed them.

Meiming hugged her relatives and followed Lydia through the white nothingness into the real word. She needed a little while to orient herself. The Head of Council was still standing where they had left her, but Nicole stood at the side with her hand on the ambassador's shoulder, who crouched beside Harm. Thin tendrils of gray smoke rose from his chest. Meiming's heart cramped. Nicole would be devastated if Harm died. She got to her feet to help Nicole when a piercing scream cut through the air, followed by the most horrible laugh she'd ever heard. Instinctively she shifted and took off, rising vertically along the castle's front. Two figures were falling toward her, and it only took her a split second to recognize them. All her blood seemed to rush to the tip of her tail. "Pa! Luke!"

Twisting in midair, she grabbed her father with her front paws while simultaneously catching Luke on her back. Upon impact, all the air was pressed from her lungs. She gasped and struggled to keep her flying magic under control. They sank with more speed than she would have liked, but not as fast as the undampened fall of the two people most important to her. The ground raced closer with every second. Suddenly, there was a scaled, white something blocking her view of the rocks.

They crashed.

"Ooof," Lydia gasped for air.

Relief flooded Meiming as she bounced off the young queen's body, even though she was forced to let go of Telanuel so she could land on her feet. His head hit the ground hard, and he slumped unconscious. Two arms encircled Meiming's throat from behind, and warm tears wet her scales. Filled with the joy of still being alive, she shifted back into human form, turned, and kissed Luke as hard as she could. Thank heavens she'd made it in time. She wouldn't have been able to live without him.

"Gosh, how I love you," Luke whispered as they came up for air. Warmth spread through her body like she'd never known before.

"I love you so much too." She kissed him again. "And you tried to save Pa."

"Not because I like him all that much." He grinned. "But I'd do anything for you."

Lydia got up, leaning against Colin and still breathing hard. "Time to wrap this up, don't you think, Meiming?"

Mordekay fumed until his blood was boiling. Lydia, Lydia, and Lydia again. That little snit ruined all his plans. But he'd show her—as soon as he got rid of the puny, annoying human that kept poking him with its arrows. Luckily his wounds healed fast, but the attacks were more than annoying. He roared and blasted the plateau with the hot flames of anger. A cry of pain rewarded him. There, that was that. He didn't bother to look how badly injured the human was. He had more important things to do.

A quick glance over the rim to the platform below told him that Telanuel hadn't died despite throwing himself off the cliff. The idiot couldn't even manage to kill himself properly. How he had stood the man was beyond him. Mordekay snorted. Just as he was about to turn away, he discovered a familiar figure. Was that the silly Chinese girl hugging the dragon slayer? How had she survived? Had he been tricked? He growled and vowed to make everyone pay. He'd make the dragons bow to his very whim.

Shifting into his human body—oh, how he hated it, but it had opposable thumbs, and he needed those—he pulled the stolen gadget from his bag and set it up with flying fingers, determined not to stay in this body longer than absolutely necessary. He had one more ace up his sleeve, so to speak, and the best thing was that it'd kill Telanuel and that idiot girl he called his daughter.

164

Very, very, very slowly the black smoke curling from Harm's chest thinned and stopped. With awe, Nicole watched the wounds close from the inside. When Luke's scream cut through the air, she wanted to help instinctively, but didn't dare to move. The ambassador was still drawing magic from her reservoir. With relief she watched Meiming jump to the rescue.

Over their heads, a dragon roared in anger. It had to be Mordekay, even though she couldn't see him, because the fiend wouldn't be far from his companion. Unable to help, she watched Meiming crash, cushioned by Lydia's dragon body.

The second she noticed that the ambassador's drain stopped, she created a net and flung it over the unconscious traitor. Then she crouched beside Harm and held his hand while simultaneously concentrating on erecting another barrier. This one she spread like a dome over the group on the landing platform. Also, she created it flexible and in layers. She didn't just want to block out Mordekay, she wanted to capture him if possible. Therefore her barrier had nets that could be detached and flung at a moment's notice.

"Ni-cole?" Harm's voice was hoarse, but he squeezed her hand with strength.

"Sssshhhh." She put her index finger on his scaly lips. "Rest a while longer. You've been badly injured."

"I must find and kill Mordekay." He tried to lift his head but failed. "He'll keep trying to destroy us over and over again if I don't."

"You're not alone." Nicole double-checked her barrier and smiled at Harm as she stroked the scales on his snout. "Let him come. We're prepared."

When Telanuel came to, he couldn't move. Something unyielding but invisible pressed him to the ground. He didn't struggle against his bonds. It was only fair that he'd been bound. Maybe the other dragons would allow him to explain himself, but he didn't expect it.

At least Meiming was still alive. How was that possible? A miracle? He didn't care. She lived and that was all that was important. Why had he lost sight of that simple truth? He felt tears roll down his cheeks as he watched Meiming—his lovely foster daughter—move to the front of the landing platform. She was so elegant and graceful. His heart went out to her, even though he knew that she'd never forgive him for what he'd done. "I'm sorry," he whispered. "I'm so, so sorry."

His thoughts turned to Sun Ling. He'd failed her so many times. How could he have used Meiming instead of protecting her? She was all that was left of the love of his life.

His heart cramped and his tears stopped as if his tear ducts had been squeezed closed. Something inside his chest jerked his heart around. What the…?

"Lydia!" He didn't expect her to react to his call, but she turned her head and raised an eyebrow.

"I think Mordekay did something to m—" The next jerk made him gasp. If his hands had been free, he would have grabbed his chest. With rising panic he noticed that Meiming was clutching her chest too, and even Lydia looked paler than a white dragon had any right to be.

"He's draining your magic." Lydia panted. "And since it's still bound to Meiming's and therefore to the realm of Queen's Magic, he's draining all of us."

Meiming toppled over and began to twitch. Lydia, too, sank to her knees, doubling over with pain, as the huge form of Mordekay's black dragon body appeared at the highest point of the castle's cliff. He bared his teeth in silent mirth and stared down. Telanuel had the feeling the black dragon was staring just at him and the twitching girls.

"Do something," Colin and Luke screamed, but it wasn't clear whom they were addressing. Frantically they tried to help Lydia and Meiming, but the two white dragons shivered and twitched uncontrollably.

It took Telanuel a moment to realize what Lydia had said. Not only had Mordekay bound Meiming's magic to Telanuel's, he'd also continued the connection until he could use both their magic whenever he wanted. Another jerk made him moan with pain. The black dragon had never been gentle. *I'll stop him, if that's the last thing I do,* he thought.

"Dragons!" Mordekay's voice filled the air like a heady perfume. Telanuel's head began to spin. *Drat, Mordekay must be using the gadget.* Telanuel swore as Mordekay's Commanding Voice droned on and another jerk went through him. "I am your queen now. Kneel!"

The dragons, still tied to the ground by some sort of creeper plant, struggled unsuccessfully to get up. Telanuel felt the urge to kneel too, but he couldn't make his body cooperate, and he didn't want to. Frantically he searched for an idea. There had to be a way to disconnect his magic from Mordekay's.

"How do I sever the bond to Mordekay?" he called to Lydia.

"You can't." Her voice was right in his head as if she didn't have enough strength left to speak. "All you can cut is the bond to Meiming."

Telanuel knew that Mordekay's drain would kill him the minute no new magic was replenishing him from the realm of Queen's Magic. Still he didn't hesitate a second. As fast as he could, he searched for the spider-silk-thin thread of magic that connected him with Meiming. When he found it, he ripped it apart with all the strength he could muster.

"Worship me!" Mordekay's Commanding Voice still echoed through the air, and though the irresistible compulsion to obey had lessened, the jerking on Telanuel's magic continued. A glance toward Lydia and Meiming showed him that the two young princesses were no longer twitching. Lydia even smiled at him.

"You've done well," she said in his mind.

"Not much longer now," he thought, not knowing whether she could hear him or not. He closed his eyes. "But at least Meiming is safe now."

When the compulsion hit, trying to force him to kneel to Mordekay, Harm refused with the loudest roar he could muster. It wasn't half its usual strength, but it seemed to help, and thinking of Nicole helped even more. He sat up, ready to take off to tackle Mordekay, when a slender figure appeared beside the black dragon. Since he was in his dragon body, Harm could make out the determination on Longbow's face despite the distance as he nocked an arrow and aimed.

Harm was airborne the same moment the arrow thudded into Mordekay's left eye. The fiend's wild roar rumbled through the mountains, and his tail lashed around, wiping Longbow off the rock. Harm raced toward the cliff, ready to catch the Native American.

There.

He grabbed the man's leg. It dislocated with an audible popping sound, and Longbow screamed. *Drat,* Harm thought. *I didn't mean to hurt him. I keep forgetting how fragile human bodies are.* He set him down as fast and as gently as he could, ready to turn around for a fight against Mordekay, but the black dragon war nowhere in sight. As he glanced back toward Nicole, she shook her head.

"No way. You're still too weak," she said. "I will handle this."

Lydia felt the drain of the magic stop and nodded gratefully to Telanuel. Tears were running over his human face, landing on the ground with low clinking sounds. *He's finally rediscovered his heart,* she thought to herself and thanked him right inside his head.

"Not much longer now," he thought back at the same time as Harm shot toward the cliff where Mordekay was screaming with pain and thrashing around.

"This is our chance," Lydia said to Meiming, who still held her chest, panting. It would be best to keep her busy so she didn't notice her father dying. "Harm and Nicole will make sure that Mordekay can't interfere again, so let's get the dragons to behave." She took the Chinese dragon's hand and together they stepped to the rim of the platform. "Open your mind to your people's thoughts," she instructed. "Then you can tell them anything you like and they'll hear it in their minds. It's pretty easy."

"But I'm not their queen." Meiming looked worried. "Do you think it'll still work?"

"You and me, we're the last royals of our clans. Since it worked for me, I'm sure it'll work for you too." Lydia closed her eyes and emptied her mind until she had enough room for the minds of the bound fighters of her clan. The cacophony was overwhelming at first, but she stilled the babble with a few soothing thoughts. Then she delivered her little speech. *Nicole will lift the binding spell in a few minutes. I hereby order you to stop fighting. We need to talk to the Chinese. Don't worry, they will not fight either.*

A few heartbeats later, she heard Meiming's voice in her head explaining the situation to her dragons and ordering them to stand back from the fight too.

"Let's emphasize that with a little bit of magic," she said, and Meiming nodded.

Nearly simultaneously they ordered with their Commanding Voice, *No more fighting!*

EIGHTEENTH CHAPTER

*O*h, the pain! Mordekay could barely think. At least he'd pushed the annoying human to its death. His hate burned like a furnace in his chest, helping him to cope. How *dare* they? He would wipe humans off the face of this Earth if it was the last thing he did. The more he allowed his hate to take over, the easier it became to push the pain aside. With a determined jerk, he pulled the arrow from his eye. It would heal eventually. After all, he was a dragon, and dragons healed most injuries in a surprisingly short amount of time. Until then, he'd bear the pain and show those imbeciles what it meant to oppose him.

Without bothering to shift back into human form, he ripped the bag he'd brought to shreds with a claw and pulled out two more Dragon Bane bombs. First he'd take out Lydia. Without her, everything would be easier.

Also, he would no longer take Telanuel into account. That weakling had too much of a soft spot for his silly foster daughter. If he hadn't insisted on using Lydia, Mordekay would never have tried to force her into a binding. It would have saved him a lot of trouble. A little bit of Dragon Bane in Angie's house and the young queen would have been history. But of course Telanuel had refused to give him the Chinese brat for a bride, and that had started the whole catastrophe. But now, the time had come to put all considerations aside. Now, he'd do whatever was necessary!

Mordekay's plan of action was easy. Take out Lydia, maybe kill Telanuel too, force the Chinese girl into a binding, and subdue all the dragons. Then they could get started on wiping humanity off the face of the world. He didn't even want them around as slaves anymore. They'd proven to be too unpredictable.

There was one more thing to do. With a little effort—the pain was still interfering with his ability to concentrate, although it had abated somewhat—he sucked some more magic from Telanuel—might as well make him pay right away—and pulled the black marble from the pouch that hid his human clothing. Juggling two bombs in one paw, he crushed the marble in the palm of his other. Immediately the witch's spell covered him like a warm blanket. He knew he was invisible and untouchable now. As a child, he'd tested the spell many times with the friends he'd had back then, a few times with the help of Telanuel too. Not even a magical barrier could stop him. This time, his plan would succeed.

As silently as he could, he took off and swooped toward Lydia on the landing platform below, holding the bombs at the ready.

Nicole kept scanning the sky. She was sure that Mordekay would attack once more, and the most likely place to do that from was the top of the castle. Holding her nets at the ready, she hoped he would show up soon. Surprisingly she didn't struggle to find the strength to focus her magic. An ice breeze from her wrist fed an unlimited amount of frosty energy into her that she could use. What a pleasant, if cold, surprise.

When Harm sped off, she had to fight her instinct to protect him. If he considered himself fit enough to rescue the lone figure falling from the cliff's top edge, she couldn't interfere. It was a question of trust. Also, her magic sensed that the falling man wasn't Mordekay.

With bated breath she stood and waited. Something was up, she just couldn't tell what. From the corner of her eye, she noticed Meiming and Lydia walked to the edge of the platform hand in hand. She extended her barrier so they were well covered again. Then she waited once more.

Mordekay would come, she was sure of that. As she watched the rim of the cliff that the castle's entrance had been cut out of, a tiny stone rolled over the edge, causing a little dust cloud as it tumbled down the steep slope. *There's not enough wind,* Nicole thought. *Mordekay must have disturbed the stone. He'll be coming any minute now.*

She lifted her hands with the palms up just as something heavy and invisible bumped into her barrier. Instinctively she let the nets fly, and they curled around the attacker.

Mordekay's voice reached her, swearing angrily. As Nicole's net strained to hold him, blue sparks appeared where her magic encountered his spell, and the whole contraption sank faster than she wanted it to. Controlling two clashing spells was increasingly difficult. Not much longer, and she'd have to let Mordekay go or risk her spell breaking free uncontrolled, and that could as well be the end of everyone standing on the platform, including herself.

No! That's not possible. I've tested it so many times. I should be able to pass through any kind of magic I encounter. Mordekay struggled to free himself from the invisible net the little witch had thrown over him. He pushed his protection outward until it built a bubble around him. Then, he reached for Telanuel's magic. It flew so slowly and sluggishly into his spell, as if the witch's net was interfering with his connection to the other dragon. Still, it was enough to strengthen his protective bubble. With the two magics pressing against each other, sparks flew, and he could finally make out the faint outline of the net holding him. The gaps were rather big. *I've still got a chance to win. Surely the witch will let go of her spell if her friend is injured.* He concentrated and aimed thoroughly before hurling the Dragon Bane bombs toward Lydia.

Two Dragon Bane bombs shot out of the net toward Lydia, wobbling as they flew. As fast as she could, Nicole narrowed the distance between threads of her nets and hurled a spare one over the two wobbly balls. If only it weren't so hard to control so many spells at once; the nets, the vines tying down the dragons, Telanuel's prison. Jerking with all her might made the bombs change direction. Nicole was insanely grateful for the strength the invisible bracelet provided. Still, it would probably be a good idea to find more options for drawing strength soon. She didn't know how long the bracelet would help, and the ground's reserves were already getting low. If she took too much, the soil would lose its structure. The whole area could collapse if she didn't find a new power source. Still, Nicole managed to direct the bombs into the brook where they broke on a rock. The Dragon Bane extract washed away harmlessly.

Mordekay howled. She felt him struggle against her net, so she tightened it around him. Strangely enough she couldn't get the net to close around his shape completely. It felt as if someone or something was pushing against it from the inside. Well, she'd have to examine that later, if she still could. Flames were dancing right under her skin. If they were alive, she'd have thought them excited at the prospect of breaking free. If much more magic entered her reservoir, she'd not only burst into flames, she'd explode.

Lydia waved to her and asked, "Can you let go of the dragons?"

Nicole was glad for the request. The soil around her was depleted and her stomach growled like a hungry predator. Only the energy coming from the bracelet sustained her. Since the sun still wasn't visible, she had no other way to gather more strength from natural resources. She'd have to move to a different vantage point soon, but Lydia's request came first.

Relieved, she released the dragons from her spell and sucked the freed energy back into herself. Since she hadn't known that she could do that, she was happy about this reserve. Without her magic, the vines turned to dust in mere minutes. The weak wind carried it away in small puffs. One thing was for sure, though: as soon as the bracelet stopped working she wouldn't be able to control her magic anymore. As she staggered forward to find an unused patch of ground, Harm landed beside her, and shifted.

"Let me help," he said and took her arm. "We still need you. Longbow is pretty badly burned, and I accidentally dislocated his leg." He pulled a chocolate bar from his pocket, ripped off the wrapper with one hand, and handed it to Nicole. She wolfed it down while simultaneously floating Mordekay toward

Lydia. If her magic failed, her friend would have to take care of the maniac.

As she stumbled forward, the ground provided some more energy. Immediately she began to feel better. Maybe she wouldn't burst after all. She colored the net green before she set Mordekay in his sphere down between Lydia and Telanuel. Meiming's foster father was still bound and lying on the ground. His breathing was ragged and his face covered in sweat. What was wrong with him?

Something delicate touched her magic net. Wait, was there a magical connection between her two captives? Could Mordekay suck magic from Telanuel or vice versa? She couldn't allow that. With a simple thought, she ripped the connection apart. Telanuel moaned and slumped, but his breathing seemed to improve. Nicole returned her attention to Mordekay and Lydia.

"I don't know why he's invisible, but this is Mordekay," she said to her friend. Then, she noticed that not a single one of the freed dragons had taken off to fight again. Whatever Lydia and Meiming had done seemed to have worked. "Is it finally time to sort out a couple of things?" she asked.

Lydia nodded, and the ambassador followed suit.

"I am sorry that our anger drove us to this," he said, blinking away tears—most likely for his son. "We should have tried the path of diplomacy first." Then he bowed to Meiming. "Would it be correct to assume that you're the last descendant of the lost princess?"

Lydia laughed. "You're uncharacteristically direct, sir. Why don't we go inside and talk things through?"

An uproar of all dragons, Chinese and European-American, made her change her mind. "Maybe it'd be better to get the

Nuciu to bring some chairs. I'm quite tired and would like to hold counsel a little more comfortably."

Since the Nuciu had to convince the young dragons in the castle to surrender chairs and stools, it took them a while to bring enough seats for the dragons and humans on the landing platform. When Nicole was absolutely sure that the fighters would remain peaceful, she removed the barrier, sucked the controlling energy of the spell back into herself, and concentrated on keeping Mordekay and Telanuel in place. Then she recreated her tendril of magic and probed the ball that kept her magical net from the black dragon.

I was as tired as if I hadn't slept in years, but it seemed the war would be over as soon as Meiming and I sorted out this mess. Grateful for the chairs, I decided to remain human and sat facing the invisible bubble laced with a green net that Nicole had set down in front of us.

Colin stood right behind me with his hand on my shoulder. It was good to know that he was still ready to defend me. Smiling, I looked to Meiming, who had chosen to shift into her dragon form. Luke was resting beside her, looking for all the world like the warrior he was. No one would guess he wasn't a man.

On my other side sat the Chinese ambassador. He, too, had chosen to remain in his human form. The reasons weren't completely clear to me. Maybe he was afraid that I could read a dragon's expressions better than a human's. No matter the reason, it felt good to have a part-time human to talk to.

"I think that we should officially end this war before we delve into the intricacies of royal bloodlines," I suggested, knowing fully well that this was a far more direct approach than Chinese dragons would normally use, but I was too tired to care much about that.

"And you have to hurry," Nicole said. "I haven't got all that much energy left to control my magic, and the soil around the platform is nearly depleted too."

"Don't you drink sunlight?" the ambassador asked, eyes wide.

"Can you see the sun anywhere?" Normally Nicole wouldn't snap at a stranger like that, which only showed how strained she was.

"We can surely do something about that. Some of us are sky dragons. They can influence the weather." He called forth an orange Chinese dragon with a yellow fringe. After a few polite phrases, he said, "Could you cause rain over the forest and sun over this castle, please?"

The other dragon nodded and withdrew wordlessly. Soon a low, melodious hum filled the clearing in front of the castle. I felt the magic behind it like a warm embrace. The humming wasn't loud enough to disrupt the peace talks, but consistent. After but a few minutes, the clouds parted and the sun shone down on the dragons and humans gathered on the platform in front of the castle.

Nicole sighed with relief and relaxed visibly. I felt better already too, knowing that the forest fires would be put out naturally. It made it less likely that humans would come to investigate. But back to the matter at hand. There were a lot of things that needed to be sorted out.

"So," I said, "the first thing we will have to discuss is the death of your royal family. I think it would be advisable if we called all dragons to the platform so everyone can hear."

"I consider that a good idea," the ambassador said, so Meiming and I did our inside-your-head talking again and called all the dragons in the forest to the castle. Silently we watched them arrive. Only when we were sure that everyone was here did I explain what Mordekay and Telanuel had done and how they'd dragged Meiming into it.

When I finished talking, she crossed her arms in front of her chest and bowed deeply. "I was devastated when I learned what I'd done. I'd never intended for anyone to get hurt. Still, I'll take full responsibility. Do with me as you wish."

Telanuel and Luke gasped simultaneously.

The ambassador smiled, an expression that softened his otherwise stern human features. "It isn't always easy to distinguish good from bad, especially when one is young. I think I'm speaking for all of us when I say that you are forgiven."

The Chinese portion of the crowd gathered in front of the castle murmured their approval.

"However, we urgently need a queen. Dragons find it hard to agree on anything without strong supervision. Am I right in assuming that you are indeed a descendant of the lost princess?"

Meiming nodded. "Mordekay and Telanuel thought they were selling you a lie, but I *am* the last descendant of the missing princess."

"Can you prove it?" The Head of Council frowned at her with disdain. "A queen truly has to be of royal blood or the realm of Queen's Magic will rise against her and destroy her whole clan. It has happened before."

NINTEENTH CHAPTER

"She is right," the ambassador said. "We need a queen who is related to the queens that came before even if the relation is a very, very distant one."

"Can I prove it?" Meiming looked at me with wide eyes, and I nodded.

"You can call your ancestors from the realm of Queen's Magic for a short period of time."

"Oh." Her eyes widened even more and a warm smile lit up her face. She closed her eyes and a few seconds later, three white Chinese dragons appeared beside her.

"Son Ling!" Telanuel struggled unsuccessfully to free himself from his bonds.

Meiming's mother arched her neck, stuck out her chin, and said. "I am Son Ling, Mei Ming's mother. I'm a descendant of the missing princess." Then she walked over to Telanuel, curled around him, stroked his hair with a paw, and whispered soothing words to him. I could tell she still liked him a lot.

Next her mother, Meiming's grandmother, introduced herself. Last it was Sun Min's turn. She rose to her hind legs so every single one of the gathered dragons could see her, and she spoke loud enough for everyone to hear her. "I am Sun Min, the lost princess. Meiming is my great-granddaughter."

The Chinese cheered, and the ambassador got up. He bowed nearly to the ground. "We are honored to finally meet you," he said.

"We are delighted." Sun Min sounded sincere. She waved at her descendants, and together they vanished as fast as they'd appeared. Meiming seemed a little sad, but the ambassador didn't give her a break.

"Would you, Meiming, consent to be the Queen of the Chinese dragons? We'll do anything to assure you of our gratitude."

Before Meiming could answer, the Head of Council interrupted. "She bonded with a human."

"We are not averse to a human companion for our queen." The ambassador stood straight again. "Dragons and humans have been mingling for a very long time, not just in China."

"The human is a dragon slayer." The Head of Council's voice sounded shrill with anger and frustration. "And a girl."

The silence following her words was immediate. It was as if everybody was holding their breath.

Luke stepped forward. "I am no girl. I'm a man, even though my body isn't. I became a dragon slayer to please my father, the man who raised me. As soon as I discovered that dragons were more than dumb, evil beasts, I ceased to be a dragon slayer. But I will be the best protector your queen will ever get."

The ambassador's face was sad, and his voice held regret. "Meiming is the last of the royal bloodline."

"I'm refusing to take the crown without him." Meiming shifted into her human form, stepped beside Luke, and took his hand.

Luke gifted her a small smile before he spoke again. His voice wobbled and he sweated as if it cost him a tremendous amount of effort to utter the question. "If I were her beloved companion, would she have to breed with me?"

"Ridiculous notion," the Head of Council grumbled.

"It would be a possibility if the queen consents." The ambassador's face didn't hold much hope. Like me, he knew better how the bonds of dragon love worked.

Meiming stared at Luke. "I'm not going to breed with anyone but you. Surely there must be something we can do. After all, we've got magic."

"Magic isn't a universal remedy," I said. Everyone was staring silently at Luke, and my heart grew heavy with sorrow. Either his and Meiming's love was doomed, or the Chinese dragons were. It was the same dilemma Colin and I faced.

Nicole noticed the tears Luke struggled to hold back. Like tiny gems, they were sparkling under his skin. *Wow, how beautiful. Magic really changes the way I see the world,* she thought, although her heart was heavy with sorrow for Luke. *If only there were an easy way to change him, but one would need a gigantic amount of magic and energy to help the two lovebirds.*

An idea flitted though her mind, and she broke the silence. "The sun is shining. That's an inexhaustible reservoir of energy. And we've got two dragons who can access Queen's Magic, a Chinese dragon who knows how to pool magic and who seems quite skilled in medicine, and a couple of dragons that haven't been drained by my creepers. With that, we should be able to adjust Luke's body. After all, it's only one chromosome that needs to be changed."

"In a billion trillion cells," Colin reminded her.

"I know it will cost a lot of magic and power, but I'm sure it's doable," she snapped. "You can't separate the two just because they can't become parents."

"To change something so fundamentally human, we would need an extremely powerful human witch," the ambassador said. His stern gaze rested on Nicole's face. "Handling so much magic without losing control of the power guiding it requires a lot of skill. If you're not up to it, it will cost you your life."

Nicole sucked in her lips. Was she ready to risk her life for her friends? She glanced at Harm. Her beloved looked just as shocked as she felt. Still, he nodded at her as if to encourage her. Did he truly understand the risk?

The flames under her skin began to itch, and she realized that she was in jeopardy already. A spell of this size was probably the only thing to get rid of enough magic so she could survive. Helping her friend probably was her only chance, because one way or the other, she was currently dancing on a very thin line between life and death. "I'll try," she said.

The silence broke and all the dragons seemed to talk at once. Only the ambassador remained silent. However, he put his hand on her arm and squeezed gently. Nicole appreciated the gesture.

She clapped her hands. "Okay then, let's get started. Everyone with magic left, stand there." She pointed to where the little brook curved around the rocky landing platform a few meters to her right side. A handful of dragons shuffled over, followed by Meiming, Lydia, and the ambassador.

Nicole drank as much energy as she could from the sun and from her bracelet and took Luke's hands. Carefully she created a tube of energy and sent it to the ambassador. As she had expected, he was already bundling the magic of the small group of dragons. As soon as her tube connected, strong magic began to flow toward her. Hurriedly she put a valve into the tube. It wouldn't do to start burning in the middle of this.

Next, she created a similar tube toward Luke. She pushed it through his hands and split its end into a billion very thin tubes that she attached to one cell each, starting at the head. The tubes smelled of sun, earth, ice and snow. She wondered whether Meiming was feeling the drain on the icy energy, but she didn't have time to ponder this for long. Then, she opened the valve and let magic flow into Luke's body. He twitched, which made it harder to hold his hands. But he also ground his teeth and tried to hold as still as possible. Nicole admired his determination.

As soon as the cells' nuclei were prepared for a reset, she closed the valve, removed the microscopic tubes and reattached them to the next bunch of cells before she opened the valve again. She repeated the process over and over again.

The sun crept over the sky closer and closer to the horizon. The support of the invisible bracelet around her wrist grew weaker with every passing moment. Alarmed, Nicole noticed that the amount of power she could draw from it began to diminish. For now, her tubes still held, but how much longer? There were still so many cells left.

She tried to work faster, but controlling the tubes took a lot of concentration. It was better to work with less speed but do it thoroughly. Something sweet was pushed between her lips, maybe fruit or chocolate, she didn't care as long as it was high in calories. It gave her additional strength for controlling the magic, so she ate. The calories never had a chance to make it into her body completely. She burned them as fast as they came in.

"Only the legs left," she panted. Even though her eyes were still closed, they burned from the sweat running over her face. Her clothes were drenched.

"Take your time," the warm voice of a Nuciu woman said and pushed more food into her mouth.

And then, the bracelet's energy faded slowly until Nicole couldn't pull even a drop from it. She felt it dissolve from her arm. Desperate, she reached for the sun, but it was already setting and didn't provide much energy. So she pulled more from the soil. It also yielded a little bit of energy, but not much. She'd already used most of this patch. *Oh come on,* she thought. *It's only the calves and feet. I can't give up now.* From Herbert's teachings she knew that if she let go of the spell now, all her work would come undone. It would rip Luke apart and kill her too, maybe even some of the dragons linked to her by the magical tube.

She chewed faster, swallowing whole lumps of whatever the Nuciu put into her mouth without tasting. Calories, she needed more calories.

Finally!

She'd reached the ankles, but the tube connecting her to the dragons wobbled dangerously. She closed the valve and dismissed it, sucking back the freed energy. Now it was just her and Luke's feet. If she could last just a little bit longer, the spell would hold.

She fed her own magic into the tube that connected her with Luke. It felt good to get rid of some of it, even though it seemed to fight more against the tube's restraints than the collected dragons' magic had done.

Two more toes. Nicole's stomach hurt so badly, she struggled to stand. *Just two more.*

Harms arms encircled her from behind. "I'll be with you always," he whispered into her ear. His warmth fed more energy into her than the food the Nuciu was still handing her. With a sigh, she drew a little more power from his warm body, knowing fully well how dangerous that was for both of them. But he'd offered, and she only needed a tiny little bit, luckily.

"I'm nearly done." Speaking was hard especially past the food in her mouth, but she managed. One final reattachment of the tubes, one more push of magic, and the last X chromosomes prepared to become Ys. Very carefully, Nicole withdrew her tube. As the last strand dissolved, she pushed a final wave of magic through Luke's hands into him, and opened her eyes.

Luke lit up like fireworks. Cell after cell flashed and changed. The chain reaction ran through his body, starting at the head. It took a full five minutes for the light-show to die down.

"You can't do unspectacular, can you?" Luke laughed at her. His voice was a full octave deeper than it had been before. Otherwise he didn't look all that much different. Sure, his face was a little more angular and his throat now sported an Adam's apple, but was that enough?

Luke grinned. "You did it. I can feel that your spell was successful, at least in the places where it counts."

Nicole allowed herself to sag into Harm's arms. She also smiled at the Nuciu woman who was still pushing fatty meat, chocolate, and pieces of dried fruit into her mouth. With satisfaction she noticed that she no longer felt the flames under her skin. She must have used up a lot of her magic and nearly all of the energy around her, but not all because she still maintained the spells keeping Telanuel and the invisible Mordekay prisoner.

Now it was up to Lydia to tell her what to do with the two of them. To Harm she said, "Let's move over to a new patch of soil. I need more energy."

I watched Luke and Meiming embrace with tears in my eyes. The Chinese dragons were cheering wildly, and the ambassador looked tired but smug. Surely this was the biggest and most dangerous magic that had ever been performed by humans and dragons in living history. If we didn't already have a chronicle, we would have to start one. I needed to talk to Herbert about that.

Herbert! Man, how could I have forgotten to alert Angie that the war had started? I turned to Colin, who was standing right behind me as if he were my bodyguard. Somehow that made me feel very well protected even though I was much stronger than he was if I turned into my dragon form. "Can you call Angie? She hasn't gotten a clue what's going on, and we'll need her here."

Nodding, he pulled out his mobile and stepped a little bit aside, just as the crowd of dragons parted reluctantly. Angie and Herbert pushed the dragons far enough aside that Blackfeather could walk through the gap without touching anyone with the wobbly, blue balloon he was carrying.

When they arrived at the platform, Angie hugged and scolded me, but she spoke so quietly that only I could hear her. "Never, ever go anywhere without telling me again. I was worried sick when you didn't come home from the ceremony." Then she turned to the gathered dragons and pointed at the balloon. "Does any of you still have one of those? They're extremely dangerous."

"Telanuel used two," Luke said. "He tried to kill Mordekay, but he seems to be immune against the poison."

I counted the Dragon Bane bombs on my fingers. The ambassador's son had one and the ambassador two. Another one was used to attack Meiming, and one for Harm. And finally Mordekay had used two. That made nine bombs. So Blackfeather was carrying the one that, according to the ambassador, got lost in the forest. I relaxed with relief. Imagine a fledgling playing in the forest and getting attracted by a colorful balloon. I shuddered and pushed the thought aside, before I said, "I think we've got them all. You can dump it into the dungeon, Blackfeather."

"Now, why isn't White Crow with Lydia?" Angie glared at the Head of Council.

"He tried to boss me around." The red dragon growled. "As if a human knows about dragons' needs."

Worry zinged through me like a flash. "What did you do to him?" Using my Commanding Voice, I ordered her to tell us.

"He's in the dungeon," she said. "He needed some time to cool off. We don't need humans to run our affairs."

A red wave of anger rushed over me as I imagined my parents' best friend stuck in the dark getting drenched by Dragon Bane over and over again. "I'm tempted to send *you* to fetch him," I told her and ground my teeth. "On one hand you want to force me to take the crown, but on the other you keep interfering all the time. I made him Head of Security, and you lock him up? How do you justify that?"

Her nostrils flared, but she didn't answer. I left it at that and asked a pair of Nuciu to fetch White Crow while I fought down my anger as best I could. I didn't want to say anything that I might regret later.

188

So I called forth the Council instead and concentrated on the other problems I still had. "We will have to mete out just punishments, and since I'm only interim queen, that's not something I want to do without your wise counsel."

"If you do not mind," the ambassador's voice was smooth as silk, "we'd love to take Telanuel and Mordekay off your hands. After all, they're the true murderers of our royal family."

I shivered at his tone and refused to think about what he might have planned as punishment.

TWENTIETH CHAPTER

*T*rying to put off the request, I said, "That's for the
Council to decide."

"No." The Head of Council shook her wings with suppressed
anger. "*You* are our queen. *You* have to decide."

Heat rose in my cheeks. "The war is over." I looked at the
ambassador. "It is over, isn't it?" Not waiting for an answer, I
continued. "I told you that I'd only be queen for the time of
war. Now I'm just me again, and I will return to Hilldale with
Colin."

"Colin over and over again." The Head of Council spread
her wings and advanced on me. "That human has too much
of an influence on you." Fast as lightning, she flicked her tail
in Colin's direction. The tip slammed against his head, and he
fell to the ground where he lay motionlessly. A pool of blood
grew around his head at an alarming speed.

No! No no no! Unable to move, I stared at the deep gash in
his skull. The blood just didn't stop. If he wasn't dead yet, there
was no way he'd ever survive this. Tears rose in my eyes. They
hurt more than tears had any right to, but I barely noticed since

the thumping muscle in my chest hurt worse. How would I ever live without Colin? The tears rolled over my cheeks, landing on the ground with soft ringing notes. One part of me—seemingly detached from the rest—marveled at the fact that I now knew how crying crystal tears felt, but the rest of me was screaming and raging. I wanted to sprint over and take Colin into my arms, but my body didn't have the strength to move a single muscle.

Angie crouched beside Colin, and a split second later, Nicole cradled his head on her lap. She was crying, which confirmed my fears. My heart turned to ice. If he was dead, so was I. I no longer cared whether my dragons would survive or not. I'd take revenge, and then I'd jump into the dungeon. It wouldn't be a nice death, but a certain one.

All my sorrow, anger, and pain exploded outward. With my magic, I picked up the Head of Council and slammed her to the ground as hard as I could. Using my Commanding Voice, I ordered, "Leave this village. You may take your hoard, but you may never, ever live near another dragon again."

The Head of Council's body convulsed and she vomited on the ground, but she got up and walked toward the castle. It took me a moment to remember that her living quarters were there.

"You can't do that," she cried, fighting unsuccessfully against my orders. "I've done everything for this community. Everything!" Tears sprang from her eyes, rattling over her dragon scales.

Crystal tears? I took a step back. She had bonded with the clan as an entity? Was that even possible? Still, it didn't soothe my anger or my pain one bit, so I kept staring at her wordlessly.

Shocked by Lydia's harsh reaction to the Head of Council's interfering, Nicole stared at the red dragon. She was too drained at the moment to help with Colin, but she knew that Angie would take care of the concussion and the laceration on his head.

The Head of Council struggled every step of the way. Only when she reached the castle's big doors, her shoulders slumped and she seemed to resign herself to her fate. Harm hurried over and called to the dagonets inside so they'd open the doors again, and while the expelled dragon walked inside, dragging her wings dejectedly and leaving a trail of crystal tears, the youngsters streamed out, loudly welcomed by their parents and other relatives.

Suddenly, Nicole realized what Lydia's crystal tears meant. She laid Colin's head down very gently, hurried over to her friend, and hugged her. "He isn't dead," she whispered. "His head is just badly shaken. Angie will heal him. She's got enough energy left."

With a hiccup, Lydia burst into tears—normal tears. It took Nicole quite a while to calm her down, and her thoughts wandered a little. It would be an interesting research subject to find out how a dragon's emotions were tied to the creation of crystal tears.

When Lydia finally caught herself, White Crow was already standing beside Angie, still wet from the hosing down that had proven necessary. He winked at Lydia, jerked his head toward the castle, and said, "Don't be too harsh on her. She is old-fashioned and narrow-minded, but she meant well."

"I want her out of the castle. And I don't ever want to see her again." Lydia wiped her tears away and looked at the remaining members of the Council. "Select a new Head of Council, and do it fast. We've got two murderers to judge."

With a face as hard as Nicole had ever seen on her friend before, she turned to Telanuel and Mordekay. White Crow and the already healed Longbow pulled Telanuel to his feet, and Nicole moved the invisible ball-like structure with her green glowing net closer to her friend.

Telanuel bowed his head, the rest of him still immobile due to Nicole's spell. "I have caused so much harm because I couldn't let go of my love. I deserve whatever punishment you choose, but please grant me a quick death."

Nicole and Meiming sucked in their breath simultaneously. Lydia would never allow someone to be killed, or would she? The anger on her face made Nicole unsure. What if the dragon rage had taken over? Would her friend regret her decision later?

Lydia turned to the Chinese ambassador. "I know that dragon diplomacy requires lengthy discussions and days of appeasing each other before any decision is made. However, I'm very tired and would like to get this over and done with. Will you promise that no one will get killed if I leave justice to you?"

Nicole let the air in her lungs out with relief. She hadn't misjudged her friend after all.

"You'd have to ask our new queen." The ambassador bowed.

"Telanuel is still my father, and I'd never kill him. Now that he admits his fault, we'll find a suitable punishment." Meiming's eyes narrowed. "I can't promise the same for Mordekay."

The ambassador bowed again. "I suggest that we strip Telanuel of his magic, leaving just enough so he can shift. That's a major punishment and will assure your safety, Your Highness."

"I like that idea." Meiming smiled, and Telanuel's eyes widened.

"I will be allowed to live?" His jaw trembled and tears streamed over his face. He stared at Meiming wordlessly.

"Well." Lydia looked at the Council. "Any objections in handing Telanuel over to the Chinese?"

The dragons shook their heads in unison, so Nicole handed her spell over to the ambassador. It was a tricky procedure because his magic was very different from hers, but after a few adjustments she was finally able to let go of that spell. She was very happy to see it go. Her stomach was constantly complaining even though Harm was stuffing her with sweets, and her whole body hurt as if she'd been trampled by an elephant. At any rate, the tickling of her magical flames had vanished as if it had never existed. Still, using so much magic at once was just as hard as trying to run a marathon without training. Herbert would have to teach her a lot more about magic soon, but at least she was no longer a danger to her friends. *Just one more spell and I can rest,* she thought and turned to the seemingly empty sphere.

"Mordekay deserves death," Angie said and helped Colin to his feet. His wound had closed and his freckled face didn't look any worse for wear. Angie pushed him toward Lydia and continued. "I know your reluctance to kill someone, but if we let him go, he'll be back with yet another evil plan."

The Council murmured approvingly, and many dragons in the crowd clapped.

"I know." Lydia lowered her head. "But I can't order his death. I'd feel like a murderess for the rest of my life. I just can't."

Colin's head still hurt a little, but otherwise he felt fine as he stepped beside his beloved. Glaring at the green net, which was all he could see, he was searching for a solution. Of course

Mordekay had to be killed. It was the only punishment that would ensure Lydia's safety. Just as naturally, he couldn't let Lydia bear that burden.

"I'll do it." He stepped forward and put his hand on her arm. She blinked away some tears and stared at him wordlessly. His body grew hot. How would the killing of a person change him, change their love? He didn't know, but what he knew was that he couldn't let Lydia do it.

"You should leave him to me," Harm said and walked up to stand beside him. "My ex-father and I have a major score to settle."

Colin felt a little guilty for being relieved.

Luke stepped beside them both. "*I'm* the dragon slayer. It is *my* job to kill him."

Colin's heart widened. It felt good to have friends like these. "Let's do it together," he said. Not that it would make the whole affair easier, but at least he wouldn't be alone.

From inside the sphere came an amused snort before Mordekay spoke. "You might have caught me for the time being, but the witch won't be able to keep up her net forever, and then…" He didn't end the sentence.

Nicole wiped some sweat off her forehead and knew that Mordekay was right. Already the threads of her net were becoming slippery. They were also thinning out. If it had only been a question of her magic, the spell would last a long, long time, but her concentration wavered and the energy she was able to draw from her surroundings was scarce.

"If only we had another option," Lydia said.

Well, to find one, Nicole would have to examine Mordekay's sphere more thoroughly. "I need more food."

With a sneer, Mordekay watched the farce taking place around his bubble of safety. As soon as the little witch's concentration broke, he'd be out of here. He regretted not taking a knife along, or he could have killed Lydia during his flight. Well, he'd have to do it another day or another way. Grinning, he shifted into his human body. The bubble tightened a little but left him enough room to stand or sit. The net took a little while to adjust its size. Not much longer and he'd be free. Mordekay smirked.

"It's a witch's spell!" The surprise in Nicole's voice caught him off guard.

What the heck did that mean?

The glowing net began to dissolve, and a light green sheen slid over the bubble's surface. Hah, he'd been right. The little witch was too inexperienced and too worn out already to hold him much longer.

The greenness spread until the whole bubble was covered by it. And then something happened that Mordekay hadn't anticipated. The green flashed. Once, twice, three times. Then it vanished completely.

"There." Nicole clapped her hands together with a wiping motion, as if rubbing him off her hands. "That took care of that. He won't get out of that spell ever unless he dies or truly repents."

"An eternity of loneliness?" Lydia's face lit up as she grinned at her friend. "That's a much better punishment then death."

What were they talking about? Mordekay walked toward Lydia. Since the net had vanished, nothing could stop him from strangling her with his bare hands. As expected, the bubble slipped unseen and unfelt over the princess, but when he reached her, his fingers slipped through her throat. What the…? He tried again, and again he couldn't touch her. He spoke the word that would collapse the safety bubble and turn it back into a marble, but nothing happened. Lydia didn't even react to his voice being so close to her. Could it be that he was now inaudible too?

Ice filled his stomach. What had that witch done? He had to flee and examine her spell thoroughly. He would find a way to break free of it, and then he'd be back. With a frustrated roar he shifted and took off.

TWENTY-FIRST CHAPTER

*T*I felt Mordekay's finger like melting icicles on my throat, but it was a passing sensation. Shortly after, I had the distinct feeling that he had left, although I hadn't heard or seen anything. For a second I felt sorry for him. Being unable to interact with anyone would become a nightmare in but a few hours. But then I remembered all the bad things he'd done, and shook off the compassion. He had to atone for his deeds or go completely bonkers. It was the only fit punishment.

The Head of Council left the castle in her dragon form with a big trunk tied to her back. Her wingtips dragged on the ground as she slowly shuffled toward an empty stretch of the platform she could use for takeoff. She was still crying crystal tears.

"Stop!" I used my Commanding Voice, and she obeyed but never lifted her gaze or ceased her crying. Still in my Commanding Voice I continued. "I've been a little too hard on you. You may find or build yourself a house somewhere and remain a member of our clan, but you will no longer be the Head of Council. And I don't want to see you anywhere near the castle unless it's a real emergency. Do we understand each other?"

She nodded weakly. Her posture didn't change but at least her crying stopped. Her voice was low but since everybody had stopped speaking, she was heard. "You will still have to become queen, and you know it."

"I refuse. You'll find someone else."

"If you don't, the clan will be wiped out," the ambassador reminded me. "We know that for a fact because it happened about two thousand years ago in Tibet, and one thousand three hundred years ago in Japan."

Nicole chimed in, slipping her hand into Harm's, who had turned back into his human form and was leaning against her. "The reason she doesn't want to become queen is that she's bonded with my brother, and these foolish dragons are too stubborn to accept that."

"But we need humans," Angie said and rubbed her red-scaled face against White Crow's shoulder. "Without them, we'd lose our ability to shift."

"That's true," Herbert said. "Settle in, everyone and I'll tell you how it came to pass that we can shift into human form today."

All of the gathered dragons fell silent. It was an eerie feeling to see so many of my subjects waiting silently for a story. A tiny smile tugged at the corners of my mouth and my mood improved considerably. It seemed that a good story could mesmerize most dragons.

I listened to Herbert with bated breath, using some of my magic to amplify his voice until every dragon nearby could hear him. Hopefully, his tale would change their minds.

"Back when most humans were still hunter-gatherers and our clan still lived in Europe, our queen visited the queen of the Chinese dragons. She was surprised to find her colleague surrounded and pampered by humans who had settled in the area around the queen's lair. Soon our young queen learned to enjoy the amenities the collaboration brought. Humans could reach itchy places she couldn't. Hunting and eating wild boar that threatened human fields fed her well and made the humans even more grateful and helpful. They polished her scales until they shone, cleaned her teeth, and filed her claws. She'd never been groomed so well. She felt rather sorry when the time to leave arrived.

"Back home, she decided she wanted human servants too. But how did one initiate the first step? She pondered this long and hard until she thought she'd found a solution. Using Queen's Magic, she constructed a human body for herself. That was far more difficult than she'd anticipated, and none of her subjects would have been able to do the same. Pleased with herself, she set out to find a suitable tribe of humans.

"She hadn't counted on them to be hostile, though. As she approached a few hunters, they caught her and tied her up. As they were discussing her fate—eat her, marry her to one of the fighters, turn her into a slave, use her as bargaining leverage for getting back captives from another tribe; the options seemed endless—one young hunter sat beside her. When she asked why they had taken her captive, he told her, 'They know you're not really human, and that's why they're scared.'

"The young queen was shocked. 'But I did my best to mimic their looks.'

"Her guard smiled. 'You forgot some essentials. Every human has a belly button, for example.'

"He explained the important parts of human anatomy and told her a lot about the way humans lived. The queen was fascinated. Since she was a beautiful woman, the young man was smitten. Thus they eloped before the tribe had come to a conclusion.

"Naturally the tribe was just as shaken as the dragons. So the two lovers fled into the mountains, where they lived. Their hearts joined in love, creating the first human-dragon bond. But to fill her belly with their children, the queen had to use her royal magic to harmonize their biologies.

"They lived hidden away for close to a year, before the human tribe finally found them and attacked them. They had never given up their hunt for the lovers.

Her husband defended her as best he could and killed many of his former tribesmen, but in the end they overwhelmed him and threw him from a rocky outcrop to his death. Although she was flying overhead, the young queen couldn't catch him in time. She cried crystal tears for him and sang him the last rites before attacking the remainder of the tribe. She spat flames at them, and no one escaped the inferno but the old, the women and the children that had stayed behind.

"The flames hadn't fully died down yet when the birthing pains began. To her surprise, the young queen still laid eggs, like all dragons. It pleased her, since the birthing her husband had recounted had seemed rather messy to her. But when the hatchlings broke from their shells, they were human in shape. So the young queen heated some stones to warm the children, turned back into a woman, and cared for them as best she could.

"Soon, the surviving women and children from her husband's tribe found her cave and joined her in an uneasy alliance. It was better than starving.

"One day, her fellow dragons showed up, demanding their queen back. So she reluctantly left her children with the humans and returned to her original duties. But when her children were grown, they all turned into dragons and returned to her mother's clan. They were the first to share human blood and with it came the ability to change shape. It didn't take the dragons long to learn how to control the shapeshifting with their magic.

"As more and more humans filled the world, their genes spread. Soon the dragons realized that it was easier to hide as a human in a group of humans than to live in the mountains, hunted by knights in shining armor. The talent became so ingrained that a shift from human to dragon and back comes like second nature now. Later it helped the last of the European dragons to flee when the humans started burning witches and anyone else who seemed suspicious." Herbert leaned back, looking smug despite his diminutive body. "You see, it is essential to renew the human blood in our veins from time to time."

When he finished, I dismissed my spell and his voice returned to normal. The whole group of dragons stared at me silently.

"Well," I said, this time amplifying my own voice. My heart thumped in my chest as if it was trying to jump right out. "I'd love to be your queen if only you can accept Colin as the king of my heart."

The youngest member of the Dragon Council stepped forward, shifted into her human form, and said, "The former Head of Council told us that your love for the human was nothing but a passing fad, but your crystal tears proved otherwise. You are truly bonded. I would be honored to have you as my queen with your human at your side." She knelt.

Another member of the Council stepped forward, shifted, and knelt also. "Me too."

One by one the other members of the Council followed their example. Soon all of them knelt in front of me with lowered heads. Cheering broke out in the crowd behind them. Dragons were calling my name, shifting into human form in great numbers and kneeling. I even heard a few call Colin's name too. Hardly daring to believe, I turned to Colin.

He smiled at me, put his arms around me, and kissed me as gently as ever. I melted in his arms, and the cheering of the dragons became a fading background to the pleasurable shivers and the happy thumping of my heart.

EPILOG

$\mathcal{M}$ordekay watched the double coronation with disdain. *That should have been my feast,* he thought, grinding his teeth. With a flick of his tail he summoned another fried chicken—not the slightest bit grateful that he was still able to summon food and clothes. He could even call his hoard for the night, but it vanished in the mornings.

Still, Mordekay was fuming with anger. No matter how hard he had studied Nicole's spell, he hadn't found out how to undo it. Her kind of magic was so very different, and he had no access to books from a dragon's library. All he could summon were novels written by humans. Not even some non-fiction. He growled as a small yellow dragon hatchling strolled through his bubble, oblivious to him.

A Nuciu ran after the little guy, picked him up, and carried him to his parents. That was one thing humans were good for. Oh, how Mordekay longed to rip Colin's throat out, and while he was at it, Lydia's, Harm's, and Angie's too.

Leaving the festivities behind, he flew back to his cave in the mountains, called his hoard, and settled down for another lonely night. He brooded. What had the wretched witch said? He could leave the bubble if he repented?

"I am sorry." It hurt him severely to be forced to say these words, as he didn't feel truly sorry, but a spell couldn't identify feelings, or could it? He pushed against the bubble but it remained as unyielding as ever.

Mordekay put his head on his paws. He'd find a way to break free and then there would be hell to pay. But deep down in his heart he knew that it would take him a very, very long time, and a wave of sadness rolled over him. An 'eternity of loneliness', that's what Lydia had called his punishment, and he suspected she was right, both about the time span and about his feelings.

Meow.

His head jerked up. A tiny, black kitten sat right in front of his snout, playing with a golden coin. Instinctively he drew in his breath to incinerate it, when the gold coin rolled out of his bubble of confinement. Holding his breath, he watched the kitten run after it, patting it with its tiny paws until it had returned it to his hoard. Then, it climbed onto one of his paws, kneaded his scales for a while, walked in a circle, and settled down to sleep. It felt surprisingly heavy for such a tiny creature.

Very slowly, Mordekay let out the air. So far, the kitten was the only creature that could touch him. Without it, he would be completely and utterly alone for as long as it would take him to break the spell. With a start he realized that he needed the animal to remain sane. Would he be able to tame it?

As he sat and watched the little hunter, he began thinking about ways to make her stay. Maybe she liked some special food. Or he could try to summon mice. Or a soft cushion. Or…

For the first time in his life, Mordekay's thoughts concentrated on another creature's well-being. And even if his behavior started out for selfish reasons, it held the seed for his redemption.

The End

A Reminder: What Happened Before

*L*ydia loses her parents and her memories in a car accident and has to live with a foster mother. When she starts school again, she meets Harm, a young dragon who can turn into a dragon. A little later she encounters Colin, a human she immediately finds likable.

Lydia discovers that she's meant to be the next dragon queen which she rejects vehemently. There reason for that is that the other dragons won't accept the love she feels for Colin.

Mordekay, a black dragon, encourages Harm, his son, to woo Lydia. He hope she'll bind with him (dragons love and bind only once). But he's not counting on hope alone. With the help of his slave Blackfeather he kidnaps Lydia, Harm, Colin and Nicole (Colin's sister, a big fan of Fantasy books), to perform a ritual that'll put him into Harm's body.

After that he wants to force Lydia magically to bind with him. But Lydia's heart belongs to Colin already, which ruins Mordekay's plan. Therefore he orders Nicole who is under his spell to pour Dragon Bane over Lydia. Dragon Bane is deadly for dragons, even in small doses. Colin manages to foil this plot and gets doused in the liquid which thankfully only results in a strong sunburn for him.

At the same time Blackfeather prevents Mordekay from taking over Harm's body. Instead he ends up in Mordekay's. Now Mordekay is trapped in Blackfeather's body.

Harm discovers that Blackfeather is his real father and not Mordekay. Together they carry off the unconscious Mordekay while Colin, Lydia, and Nicole drive home.

While Nicole refuses to believe that dragons and magic might exist, Harm has to take care of is father. Blackfeather finds it hard to cope as a dragon and can't even shift into human form. Mordekay who's now living as a servant with Harm and Blackfeather won't help. He is dead set on getting his body back, and he's got an ally.

When Harm gets injured and can't play American Football any more, he must join the drama club where he meets Luke, an A student. Since Lydia struggles with the lesons, he recommends Luke as tutor. But then, Mordekay nearly kills Blackfeather and flees. Only now, Harm realizes how much he cares for his father and the two of them finally start talking.

Colin, Harm and Lydia conspire successfully to convince Nicole that she can do magic. Since Lydia promised to visit the dragons during spring break to reconnect with her heritage, the friends travel together to the hideout in the mountains. That gives Nicole time to learn more about her magic and Harm gets a chance to court her.

When Lydia is kidnapped, the friends discover that Luke is the last fully trained dragon hunter and unwilling accomplice to Mordekay and his allies, a young Chinese dragon and Telanuel, Lydia's head of security. They find out that Mordekay and

Telanuel have a gadget that turns humans and dragons into mindless slaves.

To save Lydia and destroy the gadget, they follow Mordekay deeper into the mountains. They are ambushed and find themselves as prisoners together with Angie and Blackfeather. They can't stop Mordekay from claiming his old body, but Nicole stops him at the last moment from killing Harms father, using her magic.

He flees with Lydia's parents on his heels whom Lydia called from the realm of Queen's Magic. Telanuel is already leaving with the gadget, and the Chinese dragon follows him, carrying the unconscious Lydia. Colin is devastated and insists on a speedy and relentless pursuit.

JUMA'S RAIN
Romance-Fantasy set in Stone Age Africa

„An enjoyable fantasy with a complex heroine…" Kirkus Review

The sun's rays parch Juma as she leads her all male family toward the main village. Nothing and no one will stop her from becoming the chieftess' apprentice. So she ignores the heat. Everything will be better near the lake. But the fields that should sprout green by now lie bare, with precious soil cracked and dry. Even the lake, thought to be everlasting, dwindles.

Juma discovers that heat dæmon Mubuntu is out of control and that the rain goddess is still sleeping. But only Netinu, the chieftess' son, believes her, and he seems more interested in courting her than in the welfare of the tribe.

With her dreams going up in flames, Juma prepares to battle the dæmon and wake the goddess—and maybe, in the process, prove herself worthy of becoming chieftess.

ISBN 978-3-95681-011-4
auch als eBook erhältlich

AMADI, THE PHOENIX, THE SPHINX AND THE DJINN
A tale from the Arabian Nights in three parts

Amadi enjoys the busy frenzy the souk and tries to escape the harem her stepmother rules as often as possible. Unlike her sister Bülbül she feels caged, not protected. When Bülbül becomes engaged against her will, Amadi longs to evade a similar kismet.

Luckily a master thief wants her as an apprentice, and she grabs the chance to live like a boy. Too bad that she and her teacher become targets of a jackal-headed god of death and an assassin when they accept an assignment from a magic-using customer.

Who wants them dead so badly remains a mystery she must solve to survive. And now that she fell head over heels in love, she very much wants to live. With her life spinning out of control, will her skills be enough to save her … and, maybe, the caliphate too?

ISBN 978-3-95681-065-7
auch als eBook erhältlich

THE DWARF AND THE TWINS
SNOW WHITE AND ROSE RED
Treasures Retold 1

Once upon a time in a world where magic and technology collide with unexpected consequences…

When Martin helps a pregnant woman to flee from the king's men, he doesn't know that the twins she bears will change his solitary life forever.

What if the Brother's Grimm misunderstood the dwarf in the original tale of "Snow White and Rose Red"?

The book includes a bonus story and the original fairy tale.

ISBN 978-3-95681-028-2
auch als eBook erhältlich

Leave your eMail address so I can inform you about new releases, and this book will arrive as an eBook in your Inbox shortly after

http://www.katharinagerlach.com/readers

ROYAL SWANS
THE SEVEN SWANS
Treasuers Retold 7

Once upon a time in a world where magic and technology collide with unexpected consequences…

When neighboring royals visit the kingdom, Prince Laurent declines the princess' advances with dire consequences. Turned into swans, he and his brothers flee, followed by their sister in a flying machine. But then, they crash-land on a cemetery. Can they regain their humanity before the enraged princess catches up with them? And what about the strange ghost Laurent feels drawn to?

What if Hans Christian Andersen overlooked "The Seven Swans" part in breaking the curse?

The book includes a bonus story and the original fairy tale.

ISBN 978-3-95681-074-9
also available as eBook